P.S. You Sound Like Someone I Can Trust

ADVICE, DREAMS, AND CORRESPONDENCE
BETWEEN 8TH GRADERS AT EMILIANO ZAPATA ACADEMY
AND 10TH GRADERS AT AMUNDSEN HIGH SCHOOL

826CHI

1276 N Milwaukee Avenue, Chicago, IL 60622, USA

P.S. YOU SOUND LIKE SOMEONE I CAN TRUST

PUBLISHED JUNE 2017 BY 826CHI
© 2017 BY 826CHI
ISBN: 978-1-934750-85-8
ALL RIGHTS RESERVED, INCLUDING THE RIGHT OF
REPRODUCTION IN WHOLE OR IN PART IN ANY FORM.

THIS BOOK IS A WORK OF NONFICTION. NAMES, CHARACTERS, PLACES, AND INCIDENTS ARE PRODUCTS OF THE AUTHORS' LIVED EXPERIENCES. ANY RESEMBLANCE TO ACTUAL EVENTS, LOCALES, OR PERSONS, LIVING OR DEAD, IS ENTIRELY INTENTIONAL AND EMERGES FROM THE MINDS OF THESE WRITERS AS TRUTHFULLY AS MEMORY ALLOWS.

PROCEEDS FROM YOUR PURCHASE OF THIS PUBLICATION DIRECTLY SUPPORT 826CHI, A NON-PROFIT CREATIVE WRITING, TUTORING, AND PUBLISHING CENTER FOR CHICAGO YOUTH.
WWW.826CHI.ORG

DIRECTOR OF PROGRAMS
Maria Villarreal

PRODUCTION MANAGER AND EDITOR
Abi Humber

EDITORIAL ASSISTANT
Patrick Carey

COVER AND BOOK DESIGN
Alban Fischer
albanfischerdesign.com

COPY EDITORS
Julia Heney, Abi Humber, Patrick Carey

PHOTOGRAPHY
Abi Humber

PRINTED IN THE UNITED STATES BY MCNAUGHTON & GUNN

The views expressed in this book are those of the authors and the authors' imaginations. We support student publishing and are thrilled you picked up this book!

CONTENTS

Foreword BY ERIKA L. SÁNCHEZ / VII

Introduction BY MS. ELIZA RAMIREZ / IX

Salutations FROM ZAPATA ACADEMY'S STUDENT AMBASSADORS / XIII

IN THIS BOOK...

MAURICIO MUÑOZ & IVAN PEREZ / 3

JAZMINE RODRIGUEZ & VANESSA CRUZ / 13

   Writing Prompt: Getting Started / 24

HENRY MATTESON + MATTHEW GORSKI & SANTIAGO NUÑEZ / 26

BRYANNA GAYTAN & KAYLA MONTOYA / 39

JAVIER TRUJILLO & LIZBETH MORALES / 51

KRISTIAN DELAO & MONSERRAT GARCIA / 62

   Writing Prompt: Tic-Tac-Write / 69

AREON WHITE & GUADALUPE GOMEZ / 71

KUNJAME KHORN + ISAIAH JOHNSON & LUIS MUÑIZ / 80

   Writing Prompt: Random Word Association / 90

BRADY MATTESON & JEFFREY CORREA / 92

REUBEN RILEY & GISELLE CARDOZA / 103

ANAHI FERRER & MIA GUEVARA / 110

   Writing Prompt: Love Letter to Myself / 120

RAMÓN OCEGUEDA & BALTAZAR CAMARENA / 122

CHRISTIAN QUEVEDO & ROMAN RAMIREZ / 131

JESUS AYALA + CHRISTIAN BENITEZ & MARCO HERNANDEZ / 136

Writing Prompt: Soundtrack to My Life / 144

CHRISTOPHER RIVERA + BRYAN VILLEGAS & JAHIR REBOLLEDO / 147
SHIVAM PATEL & JOSHUA FLORES / 158

Writing Prompt: Who Am I? Who Was I? Who Do I Want to Be? / 165

SOHAIL NARAZI & INOCENTE DIRCIO / 166
CUNG LIEU & KRYSTAL NAMBO / 172
DULCE RIVERA + IVAN ALVAREZ & EDUARDO GAMBOA / 178

Writing Prompt: First and Last Thing / 189

DALILA SANCHEZ & JAZMIN ZAMUDIO / 190
SAMANTHA GUTIERREZ & ALEJANDRA ALMARAZ / 197

Writing Prompt: Identity Map / 210

FAAIZ SHAKIL & JENNIFER MOCTEZUMA / 212
ALEXA SOTO & CITHLALY BETHANCOURT / 218
DAVID POP & DANIEL NAVARRETE / 229
You! & RUTH AGUILERA / 235

ISABELLA RODRIGUEZ & JORGE SUAREZ / 240
ANGELES NIETO & JULIETA LARA / 248

Advice for Getting Through High School (and the rest of your life) Unscathed / 260

EMILY ESTRADA & ESTER ARCE / 263
EDUARDO VARGAS & BRAYAN JIMENEZ / 274

P.S. AND APPENDIXES

Post-Script FROM AMUNDSEN HIGH SCHOOL'S STUDENT AMBASSADORS / 283
Amundsen's Teacher Bios / 286

Curriculum Guide

    ESSENTIAL QUESTIONS, ENDURING UNDERSTANDING, PRIMARY READINGS / 288

    INTERACTING WITH THIS BOOK / 290

    COMMON CORE ALIGNMENT / 291

Turn That Awkward Silence Into a Conversation! / 295

Acknowlegements / 297

About 826CHI

    PROGRAMS / 301

    PEOPLE / 303

    OTHER BOOKS IN THIS SERIES / 305

    GET INVOLVED / 309

This publication is lovingly dedicated to the memory of Naome Zuber.

Naome was lost to us on October 1st, 2016, by the same gun violence that has claimed a shameful number of young lives across Chicago.

826CHI, Naome's friends and family, and her Curie Metropolitan High School community recognize that Naome's spirit is ever-present throughout the pages that follow, as young people bare their souls and beautifully share the truths of their lives.

Naome was a gifted storyteller who worked ambitiously to embolden her voice and those of her peers. She wrote authentically and with a spirit of bravery and honesty. Naome was a proud and generous young woman, author, and editor.

We miss her—and everything she was to become—desperately.

FOREWORD

ERIKA L. SÁNCHEZ

Words have the power to either liberate or subjugate. We're currently living in a world in which facts are debatable and hate speech is commonplace. More than ever, we have the responsibility to protect language. When I lose hope in what our country is becoming, I turn to young people. There I find the compassion, resilience, and honesty that is often lost among adults. I often wonder, *Why does this happen? Why do people become hardened as they grow older? How can we hold onto the trust and generosity of our younger years? What can children teach us?*

These letters between students are strong in their vulnerability. I was moved by the way these teens opened up about their lives to total strangers. There is an intimacy in letter writing that can't be replicated in any other form—the act of putting one's words onto paper as a gift to another person. This involves meditation, patience, and the genuine desire to connect. So much is communicated in these short exchanges, including the loss of a parent, the first experience of heartbreak, and various hopes and fears about the future. Some of the details these students shared really struck me. In one letter, a young woman tells her writing partner that she sometimes wears her late father's cologne, which makes her sad. In another, a young man shares about a moment at a party in which he felt humiliated. It takes so much courage to share these parts of ourselves with others.

There is a lot of joy in these letters, too. First concerts, a mother's birthmarks, a family cooking dinner together—these are just a few examples of meaningful, everyday moments and details revealed in this correspondence. They reminded me to take notice of what we often overlook.

There is so much to be learned here.

ERIKA L. SÁNCHEZ
Poet, novelist, and essayist

INTRODUCTION

MS. ELIZA RAMIREZ, 8TH GRADE TEACHER AT ZAPATA ACADEMY

Dear readers, young and younger,

I am fortunate to work with about ninety eighth graders in a public, neighborhood school on the southwest side of Chicago: Emiliano Zapata Academy. It's my immense pleasure to introduce you to these students.

You're about to meet twenty-nine of them, my homeroom students to whom I teach literacy classes. They are creative, funny, smart, quiet, socially conscious, hard-working, and thoughtful young people. I love to brag about them and tell stories of their insights and witty remarks to family, friends, colleagues, and policymakers. The great thing is, you don't have to take my word for their greatness: the evidence is in the pages that follow.

At a time in which these students are keenly aware of the ways they are vilified for being brown kids, for being Chicagoans, for being part of an immigrant community, and (for some of us) having a Mexican heritage... I jumped at the chance to have them tell others who they are and to show you, dear readers, the quality of their character. Dark times need light. This is light. *They are light!*

I immediately loved the idea of this project: Writing? Letters? With 826CHI? To older, wiser students from a different part of Chicago? YAAAAAAS! Today more than ever, it's important to meet new people, see from someone else's perspective, open up to someone different, and really listen. My students were challenged to find a connection with a stranger, uncover common ground, and share their ideas, stories, and advice respectfully. These skills are the toughest to teach and the most necessary in opening woke, contributing minds that can not only advocate for themselves, but for each other and, perhaps, the larger good of the communities to which they belong.

And the letters would be beautifully published?! We're always looking for diversity represented on stages and in pages, for familiar identities to nourish us, mirror us, and provide windows into possibility. Being published was an unexpected twist: an opportunity to be the voice *others* need, and to read in order to see *ourselves* on the page. My students—all students—deserve no less.

As you'll see, these students are just like you. They have questions. They want to be prepared for what's next. They love The Weeknd and Six Flags and will take every opportunity to tell you this. They want to live full, happy lives and have their wonderful dreams come true for themselves, their families, and friends.

These young writers are so brave, and I am so proud of their hard work. They give me hope for the future. I hope you share my sentiments after reading their letters.

Respectfully,

ELIZA RAMIREZ, NBCT
Golden Apple Fellow

ELIZA RAMIREZ is a daughter, an older sister, and an eighth grade teacher at Zapata Academy. She believes in her amazing students and their futures, for they are capable of doing anything. She enjoys traveling, collecting mugs, and reading. She would never spoil a book's ending. Ms. Ramirez loves her coffee, but not as much as she loves her students. She can't wait to see how they'll change the world.

A SALUTATION FROM ZAPATA ACADEMY'S STUDENT AMBASSADORS

Dear reader,

Hello and welcome to our book!

We are eighth graders from Zapata, and a lot of us have gone here since kindergarten. Our school has a very strong sense of community because of this, and because the teachers and staff really get to know the students. We hope you're excited to read this book of letters! Letters are more exciting to read than text messages, because they feel less shallow. You can't just reply with a picture or an emoji—you have to put meaning into everything you write, choose your words carefully, and find a way to put your personality on the page.

The hardest thing about writing this book was opening up to a brand new person we'd never met. But, we really wanted to help our letter-writing partners out with their life issues, so opening up over time allowed us to give and receive some really good advice. We also realized how much we had in common, because a lot of us had experienced the same kinds of problems. While most people might think that there isn't anything to learn from letter writing, there is plenty to learn. Some of us practiced how to be kind and gentle to new people. Others of us discovered how to write what's most important in a memory or a story. We all got more comfortable being honest about our feelings, and now feel more confident expressing ourselves.

It was helpful to have the 826CHI tutors around to encourage us to keep writing, and it was amazing because we kinda thought adults were boring. It felt nice to know that the adults were working *with* us, not looking down on us. It was also helpful to have more attention on our writing, because our teacher is usually busy teaching the whole class.

Inside this book you'll read stories about things that are important to us. You'll hear some great advice, too, and our writing will take you back to when you were in eighth grade. We hope you enjoy reading our letters, and getting to see how eighth grade minds think and feel about certain topics. Peace out and take care!

Sincerely,

MARCO HERNANDEZ
JAHIR REBOLLEDO
KAYLA MONTOYA
VANESSA CRUZ
SANTIAGO NUÑEZ

IN THIS BOOK...

Following are exchanges between an eighth grader
at Zapata Academy and one or two
tenth graders from Amundsen High School.
Students were paired up based on shared interests
at the beginning of the project,
though at the time this book was printed,
students hadn't yet met IRL.

ENJOY!

"Well, enough about you. Let's talk about me."

MAURICIO MUÑOZ & IVAN PEREZ

Dear Mauricio,

I would do a formal greeting, but I don't really roll that way, so, what's up? Answer: this is your letter. Also, I have bad handwriting, so you might not be able to read this. But whatever, I would like to know your interests. And:

- What games do you play?
- Are you into school? Probably not.
- Do you draw? Or do you just respect people who draw?
- Do you think you are better than me?
- What's your favorite music?

Well, enough about you. Let's talk about me. I'm Ivan and I'm thirteen years old, not academically achieving. I see you are a goofy guy, so I would like to ask you, are you popular for your funniness? I am.

—Ivan

Dear Ivan,

What's up, bro? I'm just bored in life right now. The weather just isn't good for anything, you feel me? Don't worry about your writing. My handwriting is also bad, but yours is readable. I play soccer, basketball, football, and you know, a lil' bit of everything. But games, as in console-wise, I don't play any. By the way, I'm fifteen. My birthday is August 1—how about you?

What do you do on a daily basis? I personally hate school with a passion 'cause I feel like it's a waste of time. If I didn't need to go to school, I'd rather work. But anyways, you know, in life, you gotta do things you don't like to succeed. How do you feel about school? (Probably the same.)

I suck at drawing, so I respect people who can do amazing drawings just from their mind. And well of course I think I'm better than you. What a silly question to ask. I am older and have more life experience in things or situations!

For now I don't like bands, but I listen to G Herbo and drill music. Although drill is my dominant type, I also like to listen to pop, R&B, indie rock, and some jazz.

Well, this is all I could write for today, but next time I'll try writing more. Deuces.

Sincerely,
Mauricio

Dear Mauricio,

I haven't talked to you since last year, ha ha ha. I would like to know, what is drill music? It sounds cool. My guess would be that drill music is probably rapping because that seems pretty popular. What kind of drill music would you recommend I listen to?

I'll attach a drawing to this letter, and it's probably gonna be about my favorite band. Maybe you could check them out. They are known as the Gorillaz. Some people might find the band weird, but it has an interesting cast of characters and they are sort of an animated band. I don't like school a lot, but it's bearable. I still have four more years of learning ahead of me, but the only upside is that I will have a job at the end. I'm not one for sports. I like to play video games and, as I mentioned before, draw.

Sincerely,
Ivan Perez

P.S. All right, I was planning on doing a drawing on the back, but I forgot about the assignment 826CHI told me to do. So, get ready for some fun facts about me!

Think of a person special to you.
My mother. She's pretty cool. She feeds me, makes my bed, and just personally helps me out with things around the house. She is a major help and she's probably the most important person in my life.

Talk about yourself!
Gorillaz! They are my favorite band. Why not? Their new album is coming out in 2017, so things are looking pretty good.

Write about the best day of your life.

I don't really have one, so instead can you tell me about your best day?

Dear Ivan,

Serious question: how do you feel about Trump becoming president? I was watching the inauguration speech at school and was just surprised that this man made it far enough to actually become the President of the United States. I really don't know why all these people would vote for a person like this. Like, he has no political background. He is a man of business and nothing but that. I just want him to disappear, or for something bad to happen to him. The whole classroom thought that too.

But what really blows me away is who knows if he's even going to do anything good as a president! The way he was talking in his speech, I just didn't believe a single word he was saying. He looked like someone who makes that salty face when they've just been exposed for telling lies. He was so unprofessional and looked like he was about to have a panic attack or something. His hands were all over the place and it just looked fake.

I personally think that he's not trustworthy, and I feel like he's going to start another war. Anyway, that's how I feel. Can you let me know your personal thoughts?

Sincerely,
Mauricio Muñoz

Dear Mauricio,

That last letter was pretty confusing because it was just about Trump. That's cool, though. I don't think that Donald Trump should be president. I think that Bernie should have been elected. He was cool. He offered better education and some other stuff.

These drawings that I make are mainly a hobby and just for fun. I don't plan to pursue any career with this. I just started off one day, drawing something that wasn't even appropriate for school, but I realized I had fun with these drawings, like drawing things that already exist and just little doodles. Then in sixth grade, I drew two drawings that were great. Seventh grade was just me drawing smiley faces like this.

[· ᴗ ·] Quite detailed faces as you can see.

Now in the beginning of eighth grade, I was just lying down on my couch and wondering what I could do to pass the time. I decided to draw the band I was listening to at the time. They are the virtual band I mentioned in my first letter, the Gorillaz. They popularized this type of virtual band and their art style really attracted me to them—I noticed that they add a lot of wrinkles to their clothing because a plain shirt with no wrinkles just looks like cardboard. It's weird, but I guess it makes sense. I cannot draw without music. Now I listen to the band that I'm drawing to get some good flow. What have you drawn that was even the least bit interesting? Do you know any people who draw well? I would love to meet them.

Sincerely,
Ivan

P.S. See you May-ish or June-ish.

Dear Ivan,

I know the last letter was confusing. That's partially my fault, but anyway, I know it's sad to see Trump as president. I also wanted Bernie to be president. I actually like your smiley faces. To be honest, they're adorable. I still haven't listened to the Gorillaz, but I'll try over the weekend. Just so you know, it's not guaranteed.

My brother is a very good drawer, actually. He paints with oils, pastels, shaded pencils, and matte graffiti. He once drew a picture of a teepee with the moon above it and a bonfire next to it. It was so beautiful, but so, so sadly for me, he gave it to his girlfriend. That's nice that you've improved over the years and that you draw to pass time.

What I do to pass time (and what I love to do) is ride my bike around Lake Shore Drive, or just take the train anywhere and explore. As long as I'm safe and outside, I am happy. I love spending time outside because you can be with people, and you don't need to worry about time because you're supposed to have fun outside.

Sincerely,
Mauricio M.

Dear Ivan,
Yeah.
           Sincerely, Mauricio.

MAURICIO MUÑOZ is a sophomore at Amundsen High School. He's a caring guy who loves being outside in nature. He does everything to live life to his full potential and hopes to achieve his dream of going to college and becoming an electrical engineer. He also hopes to win the lottery.

IVAN PEREZ is thirteen. He is a middle child and the center of attention. He can draw in a very special style. There is a band called Gorillaz, he draws in this Gorillaz art style. He plays *Streetfighter* most of the time now. He used to play a lot of *Dark Souls*, the supposed-to-be-hard-game that was beaten by a twelve-year-old seven times. *Streetfighter* is only fun when played against a player of similar skill. He is a funny guy. He makes jokes then he cracks 'em when the time is right. All in all, he just wants peace and quiet.

"By the way, you sound like a person I can trust."

JAZMINE RODRIGUEZ & VANESSA CRUZ

Dear Jazmine,

Hi Jazmine! Nice to meet you. My name is Vanessa. I'm in eighth grade. I'm glad to talk to you and get to know you better. I have a nickname, which is Vane. I am an animal lover. I love to help out animals as much as I can. I love to hear music that has a good lesson, like "Scars to Your Beautiful" by Alessia Cara. I admire her a lot. I only have a brother. His name is Victor, he is fifteen years old, and he is in tenth grade at Curie High School. Yes, I'm excited to go to high school. I'm planning on going to Curie with my brother. I live with my mom, my brother, my three dogs, and my two birds. My dad passed away.

My neighborhood is Gage Park. I don't mind that we moved here. First my mom broke her arm and then she got in a fight with my dad's family, so we decided not to live near them. I walk around my neighborhood when I'm feeling sad or angry. I can be an active reader when I'm reading an interesting book. My favorite book is *Pink*. It has a good life lesson. I only play volleyball.

I was wondering if I can also ask you questions. When is your birthday? How old are you? What are your favorite hobbies? I also noticed we have a few things in common, like our neighborhood and songs. I hope you and I have a lot in common. At first, I didn't want new friends because I'm scared of talking to people. So, it would be pretty cool to hang out with you and maybe become friends. I hope I get to know you better. It was nice talking to you. Bye!

Sincerely,
Vanessa Cruz

P.S. By the way, Jazmine, you sound like a person I can trust.

Dear Vanessa,

It's really nice to meet you too. I'm a sophomore at Amundsen High School. I'm also really excited to get to know you better.

My birthday is in the summer, August 4, 2001. I am fifteen years old. My favorite hobbies are reading and sports. I've played volleyball for six years straight and basketball for five years. My favorite author would be John Green.

I'm an active reader and I love going on adventures around Chicago with my friends, especially to the art museum. I love music too. Alessia Cara is an amazing singer. She puts so much emotion into her songs and I can relate to her a lot.

I'm really sorry about your father's passing. How old were you when that happened? How do you cope with the loss of your father?

My neighborhood is Portage Park. There are so many trees and flowers. My favorite season is fall because of all the beautiful leaves.

I would love to become friends with you, Vanessa, and to see you or hang out sometime soon. You honestly put the biggest smile on my face when you told me I sound like a person you could trust.

Sincerely,
Jazmine Rodriguez

P.S. You are a humble person and I'm so glad you feel like you can trust me.

Dear Jazmine,

I'm glad I can put a big smile on your face. If you were wondering why I didn't want to make friends, it's because I got betrayed by them. Only three of them still talk to me. The reason why they betrayed me is because they thought I was causing problems, but once they realized it wasn't me, they tried to talk to me. So, it would be cool to be friends with you.

I agree with you, Alessia Cara does put a lot of emotion into her songs. Which song of hers is your favorite? My favorite one is "Scars to Your Beautiful." My favorite part of the song is:

". . . so she's starving.
You know, cover girls eat nothing.
She says, 'Beauty is pain and there's beauty in everything.
What's a little bit of hunger?
I can go a little while longer.' She fades away.
She don't see her perfect, she don't understand she's worth it."

The reason why I like it is because the girl feels like that and I feel like that. Like I'm not perfect or worth it. Sometimes I feel like I'm useless. I wrote my favorite part on a sticky note and I put it inside of my folder. What are your top ten songs from other singers?

When my dad died I was about one year and three months old. Of course, when my mom told us, I cried for a long time. When I was small and saw little girls hanging out with both of their parents, I would get jealous because I thought it was unfair. At age eight, I realized that they should appreciate that they have both of their parents. Even though I feel sad when I talk about him, I really don't cry. This situation is something hard for me to handle. For example, I sometimes wear my dad's perfume and it makes me sad.

Your neighborhood sounds beautiful by the way. My neighborhood is just plain. It doesn't have flowers unless people decorate their house with flowers. My neighborhood pretty much just has trees.

What college are you thinking of applying to, anyway? Also, thank you for giving me a smile too because I was sad until I read your letter. So, thank you for making me happy.

Once again, I'm glad I can give you a big smile on your face, and thank you again.

Sincerely,
Vane

P.S. By the way, if you want you can call me Vane. Everyone calls me that.

Dear Vane,

I want to tell you a story about myself. I don't have a father figure in my life. I grew up missing that part, just like you. My father is alive, but he's like a dead rose in my heart. My mother got together with my dad at the age of seventeen. My father was twenty-three. She went to the same high school as me. My dad went to another high school that's about ten minutes away from Amundsen. I know very little about my father. He was never there. He wasn't even there when I was born.

Being raised by a single mother is the most powerful thing. My mother had me at the age of nineteen. She was already out of high school. My father was twenty-five. He acted as though he had no brain, no emotions. He cheated on my mother and he even tried saying I wasn't his. I've grown up thinking and making myself believe that he never existed. I'm happiest without him. My mother is the most independent woman and the way she is inspires me to be the person I am today. Do I fail? Yes, of course I do. But I pick myself up. My mother is my rock, but yes, I do wish I could be in my father's life. I wish I could be *daddy's girl*. I understand your feelings, Vane. It hurts and bothers me when I see others with their fathers, especially when they don't appreciate them. Unlike us—we don't have those father figures in our lives.

P.S. Share a story about your family that you feel comfortable telling me, Vane. I would love to hear more.

Hey Jazmine,

I'm happy for you, Jazmine, that you kept going. You are very strong because, compared to me, it sounds like you kept on. I'm very happy you shared this with me. Now I feel like I really know you and have been friends with you for a long time. Though I'm sorry to hear that your dad cheated on your mom. I know that nothing will stop you or your family.

I know we are just getting to know each other, but I hope you know that I'm here for you. Like you said, I know how it feels to have no dad. I've got to admit seeing Mom suffer taking care of us is hard. Like I told Ms. Abi and Mr. Patrick, February 10 is another year without my dad (thirteen years without him). After reading your letter, I knew I should keep going, knowing he is happy wherever he is. Like you kept going on without your father.

To be honest, I would have done the same thing and tried to forget about my dad. In my opinion, it is really hard to forget about your dad, isn't it? Once again, thanks for sharing this with me.

Every February 10, we celebrate by going to church and later lighting up some candles that we have on a small altar that's full of pictures of him. Later, we just hang out, the three of us, as if it is just us four. My mom always tells us stories about him. For example: this February 10, my mom told us that every time someone asked my dad "Are those your kids?" my dad would happily reply, "Yes, they are my kids and I'm proud of them."

So, once again, thanks for sharing this. Hope the best for you.

Love,
Vane

Hey Vane,

I'm so glad you could relate and appreciate my story I told you. It was hard to open up about him, but I know it's probably harder not to have your father alive. February 10 was hard for your family, and I want to give my respects to you and your family. I can only imagine how you're feeling—thirteen years is a long time.

Your dad is proud of you, Vane. You are a strong-minded person, and I'm gonna give you this advice: don't ever make yourself someone you're not in high school. Keep that trait of yourself going into high school. It will either make people intimidated by you or respectful of you for that, like I am. Don't ever tell yourself you can't do something or break when that's what some people want to see.

Going back to the subject of our fathers, I want you to know that, no, I haven't forgotten about him. He's on my mind 24/7, but he's also a lost memory. I only hope the best for him, but I gotta keep going and I want you to do that too. You have to strive toward what you want. Don't ever put yourself down when you're feeling sad or lonely. I can't wait to meet you, Vane, because you seem like a great person. I hope you continue becoming and growing into an amazing person.

Hey, by the way, I want to tell you a story. When I was a freshman in high school, I started dating this guy,and I completely lost my way at the end of the year. I started to care less and less about friends, school, etc. All I wanted to do was be around my boyfriend. Our relationship wasn't perfect and he wasn't either. Long story short, I found out he had cheated and I was heartbroken. It was like my whole world fell apart because I lost everyone around me. I was in a place, and a mood, that I couldn't get out of. I told you this story because I want you to be smarter and stronger than me going into high school. Don't let anybody walk all over you. Be true to yourself. I gave you this because I wish someone would've told me this: be wise and always be as humble as you are now.

Love,
Jazmine

P.S. You'll always be my best friend.

Hey Vane 🖤

Love ya TOO! 🖤
Best Friend 🖤

I'm so glad you could relate and appericate my story I told you. It was hard to open up ~~troubless~~ about him but I know its probably harder not having your father alive. February 10 was ~~real~~ hard for your family, and I want to give you my respects to you, and your family. I could only ~~imagine~~ imagine how your feeling 13 years is a long time. Your dad is proud of you Vane you are a strong minded person, and Im gonna give you this advice dont ever make yourself someone your not in highschool. Keep that trait of you going into highschool it will either make people intimidated by you, or respect that of you like I do for you. Dont ever tell yourself you cant do something or break when thats what some people want to see. Going back to the subject of our fathers I want you to know that no I havent forgotten about him. He's on my mind 24/7 but he's ~~an~~ also a lost memory, and I only hope the best for him but I gotta keep going, and I want you to do to. You have to strive what you want. Dont ever put yourself down when your feeling sad or lonely. I cant wait to meet you Vane because you seem like a great person and I hope you continue becoming, and growing into an amazing person. Hey by the way I want to tell you a story when I was a freshman in highschool. I started dating this guy, and I completely lost my way ending of freshman year. I started to care less and less about friends, school, etc. all I wanted to do is be around my boyfriend our Relationship wasnt perfect, and he wasnt Either. Long story short I found he cheated, and I was heartbroken. It was like my whole world was falling apart because I lost Everyone around me. I was in place, and in mood I couldnt get out of. I told you this story because I want you to be smarter, and stronger then me going into highschool. Dont let no person walk all over you. Be true to yourself. I gave you this advice because I wish someone wouldve told me this to be wise, and always be humble as you are now.

~~Sincerely~~
Love, Jazmine ♡

P.S · Always be my best friend ♡

JAZMINE RODRIGUEZ is a confident person. Her favorite sports are volleyball and basketball. She's outgoing, welcoming, and humble. What she dislikes are closed-minded people. She is currently attending Amundsen High School. She enjoys reading and writing. She is raised by a single mother who pushes her every day to become as successful as she possibly can be.

VANESSA CRUZ is fourteen years old. She's a girl with a mom, a brother, and no dad. She is not always nice but tries to be. She can be an angel and a little devil. She was once a shy girl, even if you got to know her. She isn't the best person but tries to be. She used to be quiet. She will become a veterinarian and a better person, but she will still be both an angel and a little devil. Vanessa loves animals, Reaction Time on YouTube, her family, her friends, and mostly: her boyfriend.

THINK OF SOMEONE IN YOUR LIFE YOU'D LIKE TO START WRITING LETTERS TO. WRITE THEM A PROMPT ON A POST-IT. GIVE IT TO THEM. HERE ARE SOME EXAMPLES:

> Hey! How's 8th grade? I know it's pretty tough but you'll get through it. I actually also read & saw 'The Fault in our Stars'. I personally really enjoyed it but I preferred the book over the movie, what are your thoughts on that? Don't stress to much about highschool, its not so bad just as long as your nice & don't try to start nothing bad, well Im running out of paper so.. bye!
> — Alexa (or naomi)

↑

MENTION A BOOK OR MOVIE YOU LIKE

> Hey Jeffrey!
> Don't worry about the letter, they told us you guys were nervous and I just thought I'd say it's no big deal. We're only 2 grades apart.
> Take care,
> Brady Matteson
>
> I do youtube too. Just so you know.

HELP THEM FEEL MORE AT EASE

> Hi my name is Jazmine. As you may know, Are you Excited About Highschool? If you don't mind me asking why did you move away from your neighborhood? What happened? Are you a Active reader? Whats your All time favoritive book? I felt the exact same way as you when I was about to start Highschool I was worried about the people to. Do you play any sports? See you soon.

ASK THEM GOOD QUESTIONS

HENRY MATTESON + MATTHEW GORSKI & SANTIAGO NUÑEZ

Dear Matthew,

Today I am going to write about something that I like to do. I like to read *Amulet* books. The *Amulet* books are the best comic books I have ever read (and the only comic books I read).

I wonder if you like any sports like soccer, volleyball, basketball, or baseball. Or, do you like any video games? Do you like watching scary movies or cartoon movies?

Other things I like are songs like "Stressed Out" by Twenty One Pilots. I like listening to the song and thinking about if the song could happen to me. I wonder, which part of the song do you like?

Well, Matthew, I think this is all. Goodbye and read you next time. I mean see you next time!

Sincerely,
Santiago N.

Dear Santiago,

I like to watch the Bears play because they're really good. Also, I watch soccer on TV sometimes but not all the time. My three favorite songs are "Hit the Dab," "I Gotta Feeling," and "Thunderstruck."

I like those songs because all of them have a really good beat. Also "Thunderstruck" has a really heavy beat that shakes up my mom's car when we listen to it. What are your favorite songs? Do you like AC/DC? If you like the band AC/DC, that is good because me and you will have something in common.

In conclusion, I hope to see you soon to find out if you like the band AC/DC and what songs you like, other than the one by Twenty One Pilots that you mentioned in your letter. Also, I hope we can be friends. What brand of shoes do you like?

Sincerely,
Matthew F. Gorski

Dear Santiago,

Hi, my name is Henry Matteson. I'm Matthew's partner in English class for the letter writing assignment. I noticed in your letter that you have a lot in common with us. For example: both of us like sports and music. In my letter, I will tell you a lot about myself.

I'm an avid fan of sports. I especially like cross country, swimming, and downhill skiing. I enjoy cross country, as I enjoy being fast and just getting a good workout. It gives me a chance to get outside and get fresh air. I get motivated to run by the terrific advice from my coach, teammates, and family. Me and Matt also did downhill skiing with our school's Special Olympics team in January. This was especially fun, as we made new friends and tried something we had never had the opportunity to do. I am also on the swim team, which is a great sport to compete in.

I have some questions to ask you as well. What type of music do you like? What do you like to do for fun? Do you have any favorite TV shows or movies? My favorite bands include Twenty One Pilots, Daft Punk, Red Hot Chili Peppers, Slipknot, and The Beatles. When not in school, I enjoy playing video games, singing, and helping cook. My favorite TV show is *Doctor Who* and my favorite movie is *The Dark Knight.*

I hope you find me to be a very cool and talented guy. You seem like a cool dude from what I've read in your letter!

Until next time,
Henry

Dear Matthew and Henry,

I wish I could write you each a letter, but I think you are both so cool so I am writing you both in this letter together. I hope you like it.

The first thing I would want to write to you guys is about my person or place that is special to me. I don't know about you, but my special person is my mom. Why, you might ask? Well, my mom is always cooking for the family (sometimes my dad helps). She gives us a lot of things and we don't even give anything to her. My mom is shy but tough. Why? Well, because when we (me and my brother) get in trouble, it is like she is Bowser and I am Mini Mario from *Super Mario Brothers*. Sometimes I win in the video game, but in real life it is always like GAME OVER. My mom makes the most delicious food and I smell her cooking every day. YUM! When she makes beans you have to step two feet away from my brother. (I actually don't mean this in a mean way.)

Another thing that I am going to be talking about (well, actually, writing about) is what freedom means to me. To start this up, I think freedom means to me that you can do anything you want. Once on a dark, dark night, me, my brother, and my little sister were in my room playing Wii. My mom was sleeping in her bed and we got to play alone. I think that was freedom.

Do you both like video games? If you do, which ones? Do you have consoles? Do you like music? How about Legos? I can't think of any more questions. Read you next time.

Sincerely,
Santiago Nuñez

"When me and my brother get in trouble, it is like my mom is Bowser and I am Mini Mario."

Dear Santiago,

I have a lot to tell you about high school and my experience skiing on my school's ski team with the Special Olympics. It's really fun because you get to ski down hills really fast, and you do it with kids just like you who have disabilities too. That is what makes it fun. The coolest part is when you get a medal, and the medals are very shiny and very cool looking. I have never fallen on skis before when going down a hill in a competition, but I have fallen during practice.

Have you ever been bullied at school before? I used to get bullied at school and it was not fun. It also hurt me inside and made me extremely angry. If you get bullied at school, I understand how you feel.

I hope you meet me in person so I can talk to you, so we can be friends, and so I can walk around with you in the hallways of Amundsen.

Sincerely,
Matthew F. Gorski

P.S. I won three medals skiing this year in the Special Olympics!

Dear Santiago,

I have an interesting story to tell you today! It's about how I won a gold medal in downhill skiing. I will explain how even if you aren't the best at something, you can practice and keep trying to get better. Follow me down the slopes as I tell you how, with enough practice, you can achieve anything!

It began in January 2016. I was on my way to the Chestnut Mountain Resort in Galena, IL. It was my first day skiing with my school's Special Olympics Ski Team. After a three-hour-long bus ride of eternity, we made it. Within an hour, I would be skiing! The first challenge, however, came when we were getting into our ski gear. Getting on the bundles of clothes was okay, but it was the boots that were the main challenge! After getting bundled up, we walked down to the equipment room, where the boots and skis were. Me and my teammates Matt, Noel, and Henry all struggled to fit the boots on! After help from coaches Mr. Ward, Mr. Craig, and Mr. Binder, we learned how to walk in the boots. Boy, was it painful. They were heavy and felt like they were made of lead! After that, we learned how to take our skis off and how to fall. Both were equally a bit challenging, but getting up took a while, as we had to slowly move our arms backwards and walk backwards to get up.

Then, the second day came along. That day we learned how to do a "pizza" with our skis to slow down and "french fry" to go fast. We went down the Bunny and Rookie's Ridge trails. Going down the hills and learning how to slow down was a breeze for me. I also learned how to turn, which I wasn't as good at. I kept crashing and nearly hurting others! However, after getting help from Mr. Ward and Mr. Craig, I slowly got better. I even got to do down a bigger hill. It was kind of scary, but I'm used to it now. After a long day of skiing, we were just one day away from the competition.

After an exhausting day and a night of restless sleep, the competition was finally here. I was confident that I would win some gold. Me, Matt, Noel, and Henry were all a little nervous, but we all hoped to go on to the championships. We all were allowed an hour of practice before the games began, so I went over to my usual Rookie's Ridge trail for a few laps. Mr. Ward, Mr. Binder, and Mr. Craig were all confident we'd do great!

When I was ready to compete, I got a little more nervous, as I felt I was going to do badly. However, after racing down and avoiding the colored flags, me, Matt, and Henry made Amundsen proud by winning gold! Unfortunately, Noel didn't qualify, but we still cheered him up and told him he did great anyway. In the end, I've learned that with enough practice and confidence, you can achieve anything!

Sincerely,
Henry Matteson

Dear Matthew and Henry,

Some weeks ago in a school not very far away, it was Valentine's Day. And on Valentine's Day, we had a dance. Do you guys have a dance when it is a holiday?

My Valentine's Day started fine. I usually come late to school and I forget things and my day is not the greatest, but this day started okay. It was Tuesday, so I knew 826CHI was coming to write with us during literacy class. Time passed fast with them in our class, then I had to finish my social studies project on the computer before I could go to the dance. Then Ms. Ramirez said, "Okay, students. Line up." I checked the clock: 1 p.m. The dance! I was almost done with my project—only two more sentences and then, I was finally done!

I was happy because at the end of the hall I could hear the loud music coming from the gym. Outside, I saw my classmate Balta and he told me, "Crystal is waiting for you." I said, "Okay, thanks." When I went inside the gym, the music was even louder. I asked my friends Jacob and David if they'd seen her. "Nope," they both said. A few minutes later, my brother came toward me. "Hey, bro." I had totally forgotten about him. He was with our neighbor, Heriberto. Heriberto is a cool kid. I couldn't find Crystal, so for a lot of the dance I was mostly hanging out with my brother and Heriberto.

I finally found Crystal, and we got to talk and dance for what felt like five minutes. I did not bring the card that I was going to give to her. Instead, I bought her candy. It went fine for me. Oh, I forgot to tell you: if you were wondering who Crystal is, she is the girl who I've been going out with for three weeks.

See you in June, I think.

Sincerely,
Santiago Nuñez

Dear Santiago,

I think it was very cool and brave that you were able to dance with Crystal. I was never that brave in eighth grade. The one time I was brave was when I sang and performed with my school's rock band. I had to work up a lot of courage to sing, but I had a ton of fun, even with a couple of mistakes.

This was in eighth grade, a month before I would graduate from middle school, and it was the day of my school's variety show. One of the performers was the school rock band, for which I was one of the singers. We'd been practicing for months. I got to sing on a couple of songs, "Sunshine of Your Love" by Cream and "Do I Wanna Know" by the Arctic Monkeys. I typically get nervous singing on stage, but I felt a lot more confident that day.

It was showtime and I was on stage, singing casually for the first song with two other singers who were sharing a mic. It was a little uncomfortable because the stage was so small. Then, on the second song, the other mic broke! I was the only one singing. I quietly and nervously sang more of "Do I Wanna Know," but remembering that the show must go on, I gathered confidence to continue singing! By the end, I felt a lot more relaxed and the crowd even cheered me on, seeing that I sang bravely no matter what happened. What do you think of my story of bravery? To answer your question about if Amundsen holds holiday dances, the answer is no. However, we do have fun homecoming and winter dances! Hope you are well!

Henry Matteson

P.S. Good job again on dancing with Crystal! :)

HENRY MATTESON is a fifteen-year-old from Chicago who attends Amundsen High School as a sophomore. He enjoys participating in his favorite sports, which include swimming, running cross country, and competing in the Special Olympics, for which he holds an impressive two gold medals! Outside of school, he loves listening to rock music, cooking, reading, and practicing guitar. In the future, he would like to be a chef, like Gordon Ramsay, except without getting mad or yelling at other chefs!

MATTHEW F. GORSKI goes to Amundsen High School and is sixteen years old. He is a very strong person who loves dogs. At home, he lives with his brother Dan, his mom, and his dad. He also loves to read and ski. Other people like Matthew because they know that he is a kind, strong, and nice young man. He is also a good reader and writer. At school, he is a very hard worker every day. He was a person who got bullied at school a lot, but that is done and he is now very liked at school. Matthew is very athletic and very strong.

SANTIAGO NUÑEZ is a shy student who likes to watch, play, and read about Star Wars. He spends his time playing Five Nights at Freddy's. He is also a Minecrafter. He plays with his brother and friend. When he grows up he wants to be a video game maker or an actor. When he was little he was a kid, he didn't like to read. Now he has a lot of books he can read with his friends and family.

"I see that you happen to enjoy reading, as you have 214 of your own books."

BRYANNA GAYTAN & KAYLA MONTOYA

Dear Bryanna,

Hello! How are you?! I hope you're happy and content with things. I see that you happen to enjoy reading, as you have 214 of your own books. I too have been reading since I was small—five years old. I used to read with my mom when I was small. It was really nice. Of course, my small collection of books does not compare to yours of 214, but I have some.

My favorite book is *Carry On* by Rainbow Rowell. Have you ever heard of it? It's really descriptive and magical, and I would recommend it. The book before *Carry On* is *Fangirl*, which is also pretty good. What's your favorite book?

I also saw that you're into anime. I am too! My favorite anime is *Owari No Seraph*, truly iconic. What is yours? I actually have gotten out of anime and transitioned into K-pop. I currently love BTS, a great group in my opinion. It's a group of seven members. What kind of music are you into?

This is getting sort of long—I'm sorry. I hope you're well and that your day is amazing! Hope to hear from you and learn some things.

Sincerely,
Kayla

Dear Kayla,

Hey! I was so happy to read your letter. To answer your question, I've seen *Carry On* at the store before, but I've never read it. I've seen *Fangirl* too. My favorite book is probably *Diary of an Oxygen Thief*. I love that we can relate over how much we love books.

I'm into a lot of different music, especially old school R&B, like Kanye, NWA, Dr. Dre, stuff like that. You should totally tell me more about your family, I'd love to know! I can start: I have a younger brother and sister. Sorry my letter is so short, but I really hope you are doing well. I hope to hear from you soon!

Sincerely,
Bry

Dear Bryanna,

I enjoyed reading your letter. Thank you for taking the time to read mine and respond to it. While writing this, I am so happy about being able to get tickets to see BTS perform in Chicago! It makes me really happy knowing that I will be able to see them in person and not just through a screen. After seeing Bangton for so long, they begin to seem unreal and so distant. I happen to really love music, especially a song where you can really feel the beat and the rhythm. Music is always a go-to for me, it can make my mood go from zero to one hundred. I hold music very close to my heart.

Something else I hold close to my heart is my older sister Bianca. Bianca and I have a very close bond and relationship. She always comes to me when she has problems with her boyfriend and other things. We are very playful with each other and can always make each other laugh. She's like my other half. Though we used to fight tons when we were smaller, we have bonded a bunch since then and have gotten much closer.

Who is someone you hold close to your heart? Have you ever had some wild times with your siblings? When I was smaller, I was mad at my sister for some reason. She had been sharpening pencils and so I took one from her and stabbed her with the pencil! Of course, I was small and didn't know what the outcome would be, but that really happened! I love my sister to pieces and would never try to hurt her on purpose. Another time, my sister got mad and kicked me in my stomach. It shows how much we used to fight, but also how we've matured together. How is your relationship with your siblings? I hope your day goes well (when you receive this)!

Sincerely,
Kayla

Dear Kayla,

Hi! It's great to hear back from you. I'm so excited for you about seeing BTS in person! Concerts are so much fun. I've only been to two my whole life sadly :(. But I've been trying to save my money to see The Weeknd in concert on May 27. Your letter was so cute and I'm so glad you have such a good connection with your older sister. Those type of connections are the best. It's like having your BFF live with you. I'm the oldest of three, my brother is eight and my sister is two. We're all like super crazy close though, for being so far apart in age. And yes, pretty much every time I'm with them it's pretty crazy because they're so young and hyper!

For these letters, how about I tell you some things about myself and my life? Then when you write back, you can do the same and that way we get to know each other a little better. So, hmm, well, you already know I'm the oldest of three. I live with my dad. I play soccer, volleyball, and basketball. I LOVE Thai food even though I'm full Puerto Rican. I'm not sure what else. I guess I'm a pretty boring person after all.

I love school, though not the learning and being in class all day part. Seeing my friends and boyfriend, and not sitting in my house all day, is fun to me. High school is so fun—you're going to love it! Freshman year was way more fun than this year so far. Freshman year, the classes are easy, you make new friends and just have a lot of fun. I made so many new friends and met my boyfriend last year. I hung out after school all the time, so I was barely home. One piece of advice about high school that I can truthfully give you is that your old elementary school friends may or may not stick around when you're all in high school. Most likely, they will not. I had been BEST friends with a group of four girls since the first grade, but now that we're at different schools, we don't even text or talk anymore. But it's okay. I met even better people who love me and won't let distance get between us.

That's basically it, kiddo. You lose some, you win some. Sorry I wrote so much. I felt like I owed you after your awesome letter, and since my last one was so short :(. I love ya, Kayla. Write back soon!

Bryanna ♥

Hey Bryanna!

I hope you've been feeling well and that you've been able to enjoy yourself. About high school and the friend thing, I think I have one friend I can count on to keep in touch with me even after we've gone off to high school. Her name is Nicole and she means tons to me. She and I have been friends since second grade. Though the amount of time we've been friends might not matter to some people, it surely means something to me. She was the whole reason I even got tickets to see BTS in the first place! I'm so thankful to have her as a friend.

She is a precious angel. I once went over to her house and we just hung out on her roof listening to music. Things like that make me happy. Someone you can hang out with, just listening to music and having fun with, is someone you should never let go. I have never grown tired of her. Nicole and I have even had six whole GBs worth of text messages—I love Nicole! One time she and I were talking, and she said she would not allow us to drift apart. I love that I have someone who can even tell me that in the first place. Though I might sound young and naive to you, Bryanna, I believe we'll stay in touch.

Middle school has been wild for me. In my English class (when 826CHI comes) I sit with my classmates named Jennifer, Inocente, and Daniel. They are all very fun to be around. Daniel is a good storyteller, occasionally making jokes between stories. He can make even the grumpiest of people laugh. Jennifer is generally quiet, but depending on who she's around, she can become very loud and giggly. Inocente is very quiet, but he's pretty funny if you listen close and ever catch one of his jokes. Together we all blend well and we love making each other laugh.

I also have another friend named Jen and I love her so much! Jen is very funny, but also very relaxing and refreshing. She's very good with emotions and helping others. It's amazing, like, how she is even REAL?! I am terrible at comforting people when they're upset, so it is amazing to see someone like Jen as an actual, walking, breathing person who can do that.

All in all, I cherish all my friends very much and would love to keep in touch with them, but I obviously can't expect so much from everyone, like you said. Whether we stay in touch or not, I know I will definitely not forget all the nice things they have done for me and I will cherish all the beautiful memories. I hope you yourself have great friends and memories that you can look back at and smile. I hope you have been enjoying yourself and that you like reading my letter.

I wish you all the best! Until next time, Bryanna.

Sincerely,
Kayla

BRYANNA GAYTAN is fifteen years old, will turn sixteen in April, and lives in Chicago. She plays soccer and volleyball. She wants to go to cosmetology school after high school. Her best friend's name is Sam. She's also in this book. Bryanna loves school, but not the learning part. She has a heart tattoo on her right leg, as does her best friend. She loves meeting new people. Her favorite book is *An Abundance of Katherines*.

KAYLA MONTOYA is a thirteen-year-old girl who lives in Chicago. She enjoys lame Twitter memes like "What in Tarnation" and dancing in the mirror while listening to music. Kayla loves to read, especially *Carry On* by Rainbow Rowell. Kayla is lame and keeps a journal just to write random things and adds pieces of magazines to it. She enjoys family, friends, and flowers.

SIX-WORD MEMOIRS

Here are some examples from the students in this book:

Constantly increasing my to-read list.

I love to draw really good.

I don't like family vacations anymore.

School was easier when I was younger.

Showing who I am is hard.

I will write my memoir tomorrow.

HERE ARE MINE:

"I love shopping, and I like to be honest with people."

JAVIER TRUJILLO & LIZBETH MORALES

Dear Javier,

My name is Lizbeth and I'm thirteen years old. I live in Little Village. I come from Mexican parents, and the most important thing to me is my family. I love shopping, and I like to be honest to people. I was born in Chicago, Illinois. I go to a school named Emiliano Zapata Academy. I listen to music but not all the time. I have friends but not a lot. I have three friends. My neighborhood is great. I have fun traveling in my neighborhood. I like to travel in Mexico. It is one of my favorite places to travel, and I have a lot of fun there.

Well, now I want to ask you some questions! Where are you from? What is your favorite thing to do? What is the most important thing to you? Do you like your school? What is your favorite subject? Do you like to read? What places have you travelled to? Do you like sports? Well, those are the only questions I have for you. I hope this will be enough information about me.

Sincerely,
Lizbeth Morales

Dear Lizbeth,

My name is Javier Trujillo and I'm sixteen years old. I live in a neighborhood called Albany Park. I have lived most of my life in Albany Park. I came from Mexican parents and I'm the only child in my family that was born in Chicago. My parents and my older sister were born in Michoacán, Mexico. To be honest, it's pretty stressful being the first child to be born in Chicago and in the United States because my parents expect more from me. They expect me to get a better education, a better job, to get into a great university, and to get a good degree. And I know I might sound stereotypical, but I love to play soccer and I'm on my high school's soccer team. I've been playing since my freshman year.

To answer some of your questions: my favorite activities would consist of sports, music, and art. I play soccer, football, softball, volleyball, and basketball. My favorite sport would be soccer. My position in soccer would be right wing or center right midfielder. I love running around and helping out on defense, but I love going up to score, as well. I love the adrenaline I feel while I'm dribbling around the other players. It's just amazing contributing to a "big family." Joining a program in high school is great when you need support and people to relate to. They will be your family throughout your high school experience.

High school is overall an amazing experience. You learn a lot in your classes and you meet amazing teachers. If you have any more questions, I'd love to answer them.

Take care,
Javier Trujillo

Dear Lizabeth,

My name is Javier Trujillo and I'm sixteen years old. I live in a neighborhood called Albany Park. I lived most of my life in Albany Park. I came from Mexican parents, and I'm the only child in my family that was born in Chicago. My parents and my older sister were born in Michoacan, Mexico. To be honest it's pretty stressful being the first child to be born in Chicago and in the United States in general, because my parents expect more from me. They expect me to get a better education, a better job, and to get into a great university and get a degree. I know I might sound stereotypical, but I love to play soccer and I'm in my high school's soccer team and I've been playing since my freshman year.

To answer some of your questions: I'm from Chicago, Illinois. My favorite activities would consist of sport, music, and art. I play soccer, football, softball, volleyball and basketball. My favorite sport would be soccer. My position in soccer would be right wing or center right midfielder. I just love running around and helping out defense but going up to score as well. I love the adrenaline while I'm dribbling around the players. It's just amazing contributing to a "big family." Joining a program in high school is great when you need support and people to relate to. They will be your family throughout your high school experience.

High school is overall an amazing experience to take. You learn alot in your classes, you meet amazing teachers, but if you have anymore questions, I'd love to answer them.

Take care,

Javier Trujillo

Dear Javier,

I got your letter and thank you. It was fun to read it. I like how you answered my questions. I noticed we have some things in common. I read that you like volleyball and I also like to play volleyball. It is one of my favorite sports. I also read that you like soccer. Cool, that's a good sport. You exercise a lot. I do like soccer but not that much. My two brothers like to play soccer. My parents are also from Mexico, like yours. Also, my parents want me to have a good education and have a better job in the future.

The best day of my life was when I went to Mexico. Mexico is really different from Chicago. Mexico is like another world where you feel free. You can't compare Chicago to Mexico because they're so different. They might have some things in common but not that much. When I went to Mexico for the first time, I didn't know what to do because it was a new place for me, but as the days passed I went to different, fun places. There was a store where they had machines that you could play video games on. Everyday I wanted to go to the store and play my favorite machine game. That was my favorite thing to do in Mexico and I will never forget it.

Okay, now I'm going to talk about a special place for me. It is my home because it reminds me of happy moments with my family and also the saddest moments. It also reminds me of my two brothers and sister growing bigger. When I see my house, I immediately remember all these things. Well, that's it. If you have more questions for me, I would be happy to answer them.

I do have some questions for you. What is your favorite color? What is your favorite food to eat? What is your favorite thing to do in your free time? I hope you have enjoyed reading my letter.

Sincerely,
Lizbeth

Dear Lizbeth,

I enjoyed reading your letter. I love tacos! They are my all-time favorite! Well, a lot has happened throughout these couple of weeks. I'm a family person, so I'm always with my family and really get along with them. Actually, one of my uncles died and it was a pretty harsh to experience to go through. I also ended up in the hospital on another night and, well, the news didn't excite me. I found out that I might have a heart condition that could lead me to death, but the doctors referred me to a cardiologist. They are going to run some tests and figure out if I'm having that condition for real or if it was a one-time thing.

I have had a lot of free time and since I couldn't workout or play soccer, I started to write. Not just because it was a homework assignment—it was something I wanted to do. I'm not much of a writer and I didn't know what to write, so I wrote a story. Hopefully, you'd like to read it. I would like to know a story about your family or you—the most memorable, the craziest, worth-talking-about story. I'd honestly love to hear about it!

Javier Trujillo

Dear Javier,

I enjoyed reading your letter. I'm also a family person. I'm always with my parents, but it doesn't bother me, being all the time with my family.

I'm so sorry that you went through all of this and that your uncle passed away. I haven't been through this, but I can imagine how bad it feels to lose somebody you love. I hope you feel better and your family too. I wish nothing bad had happened. I'm sorry about your heart condition and I hope you are better soon.

I do have one experience that I can't forget that I will tell you about: The first time I went to Mexico, it was on a bus. I was really nervous because it was my first time. I didn't know how Mexico would look or what it would be like. But I can't forget it because of the bus. It is so horrible to ride on a bus for almost three days. It felt horrible because it was hot outside and all the people in the bus made it hot too.

At first, I didn't want to go to Mexico because I didn't know people there, but when we got there it was so cool. You can feel free. When I got there, so many kids were playing. I got to meet a cousin of my same age and another cousin only one year older than us. When it was time to go back, I didn't want to go because I loved Mexico.

Sincerely,
Lizbeth

Dear Lizbeth,

I appreciate your worrying and hoping for the best for me and my family. Lately things have been calm and are getting better. I went to the hospital for an appointment and the doctor told me that I'll be all right. My heart is stable and I won't suffer drastic effects. I honestly felt so relieved to hear that I am stable. The very next day, I got up earlier than usual. I went for a long run and played soccer like never before. I was so worried that I wouldn't get to return to heavy weight training and intense workouts, but I just picked up from where I left off and I'm gradually making progress.

Mexico is such a beauty. Roaming Los Ranchos and the little cities is a must. I remember that my family over in Mexico would take me to Morelia to go shopping and to this water park. Because there are mostly females on my mother's side of the family, I play soccer or juggle the ball if I get bored.

My fondest memory would be when I bought my fixie. Once the package came in the mail, I built the bike myself and rode out. I always ride downtown and to the South Side. It takes an hour or two, but it's totally worth it. I've learned many routes and new places. I always try to revisit them when I can. I would bring my older sister, but she's too slow to ride with me.

I don't really have any other specific questions, but I'd love to hear any other story you're willing to share.

Sincerely,
Javier Trujillo

P.S. During my bike rides I usually witness the east shore of Chicago, like the Lake Michigan scenery. For example, I rode out with a friend this Saturday night on the Lakefront Trail, down past the Bean and the Willis Tower. After riding to the Bean, we cruised downtown. We were just enjoying the view and trying to take as many pictures as we could. The Lakeshore Trail is my favorite route. It's lengthy, but it's a lot of fun. You get to witness nature, the lake, the Chicago skyline, and it extends way down to the South Side. I just love it.

JAVIER TRUJILLO is sixteen years old. He was born and raised in Chicago. He is Mexican American but was raised as a full-on Mexican. He loves to play volleyball, softball, baseball, and soccer. Some other interests are music, art, and food. Javier loves tacos! *Buy him tacos.*

LIZBETH MORALES is thirteen years old. She goes to Emiliano Zapata Academy. She loves to spend time with her family, and has two brothers and one sister. She likes to go to Mexico. She's a shy person. She would like to design clothes, be able to cook different kinds of food, and be a doctor or a nurse.

KRISTIAN DELAO & MONSERRAT GARCIA

Dear Kristian,

Hi, I am Monserrat, but I prefer to go by my nickname, Monse, since that's what everyone calls me. I'm an eighth grader at Zapata Academy. I'm really quite shy at first, but once you get to know me I might be goofy and loud. I laugh a lot sometimes. My birthday was a few days ago, so now I am fourteen years old. When is your birthday? How old are you?

Can we just talk about how I can relate to you about waking up and just taking my time for everything: waking up, dressing, and eating my breakfast. Because I take so long, I almost end up getting a tardy slip every day. I just live like three blocks from school! (I know, that's bad.) I am going to be completely honest, I only get all girly when I fangirl over someone, *cough* Shawn *cough* Mendes. I feel like he is the only pop singer I listen to. I either listen to Spanish music, hip hop, or R&B. Who is your favorite artist? What genre of music do you like? During my free time I always read, text, or just watch TV series on Netflix and also YouTube videos.

I wanted to share the best day of my life with you: the day my baby brother was born. I am going to be honest with you. Before, I wasn't so happy about the idea of having a little sibling. I mean, I already have my sister and having someone new in the family didn't really make me happy. Now, I love him to death. He is four years old and I really love him, even if he can be really annoying at times. Do you have any siblings? Actually, I am the oldest sibling, which has its pros and cons. It's great since you can be the first to do certain things, but it's hard because your younger siblings look up to you, so you have to try not to do anything bad.

Well, I don't know much about you, so I hope to hear more about you.

Sincerely,
Monserrat Garcia

> Dear Kristian De Leo
>
> Hi I am Monserrat, but I prefer to go by my nickname, Monse, since that's what everyone calls me by. I'm an 8th grader at Zapata Academy and I'm really quite/shy at first but once you get to know me I might be goofy and loud (sometimes) yeah and I laugh a lot sometimes. Well I am 13 yrs old soon to be 14 in December 30th. When is your birthday? How old are you?. Can we just talk about how I can relate with you with waking up and just taking my time for everything, like waking up, dressing up and eating my breakfast and because I take so long I almost end up getting a tardy slip and I just live like three blocks (I know. that's bad). I am going to be completely honest I only get all girly when I fangirl or something or someone *cough* Shawn *cough* Mendes. I feel like he is the only pop singer I listen to I either listen to spanish music or hip hop and R and b. who is your favorite artist? what genre of music do you like. well I don't know much about you so I hope to hear about you.
>
> Sincerely, Monserrat Garcia

Dear Monserrat Garcia,

Hey, I'm Kristian. I am a tenth grader at Amundsen High School and I am sixteen years old. Happy late birthday to you! I am also really shy with new people, but then once I get to know them and be comfortable, I am myself and also kind of goofy. For me, it takes about a couple weeks to get to know people and get comfortable around them. I don't really have a favorite artist, but the person I listen to the most would probably be Drake. My favorite music genre is rap. For me, what I do in my free time is play sports, mainly basketball.

I do have siblings. I have a younger brother and an older sister. I wish I was the older sibling because it sucks being the middle child. My younger brother and older sister always get what they want, but I rarely do.

One thing that I wanted to share about myself is that I am from Belize—well, my parents are—even though most people think I'm from Mexico. Not a lot of people have heard of Belize, or they don't know where it is. It's in Central America, next to Guatemala. I've never been there before, but I heard that it's a really beautiful place and I've seen a couple pictures.

Anyway, I want to know more about you. Where are you from? What kind of talents do you have? Do you know what career you want in the future? Can't wait to hear back from you.

Sincerely,
Kristian DeLao

hurry up & wait

as it happens
the moon comes
& goes
glows & dims
whether you
stress out
or not

let the crazy
blow on by.
be the still chill
at the center
of the hurricane

the arc
of life is short,
too short
to miss
a single heartbeat

the notorious e.r.p.
poems while you wait
826chi prologue
6.9.17

Eileen Jones

Dear Kristian,

I can totally relate with the Drake thing. I literally listen to him 24/7 and I don't get tired of his voice. My favorite song from him would be "Best I Ever Had," apart from "Fake Love." Which is your favorite Drake song? Netflix is life, to be honest. I am currently watching *The People v. O.J. Simpson*. I really recommend it if you haven't watched it, since it's based on a crime story—a real one.

Both my parents are from Mexico, so I am Mexican American. My Spanish is okay. Being Mexican American has its pros and cons. The con is that people (some) will judge you for your race. The pros are that our family is big and we have a great bond, not to mention the food. I have gone to Mexico once, but I was only two years old so I don't remember. I really want to go to Mexico again just to visit but also to go see my grandpa since I don't see him much. What are two places where you want to travel?

I don't think I have a talent, but when I grow up I want to be a pastry chef. I have not tried to cook anything, but I watch so many YouTube videos. For high school, I applied for culinary arts. What's high school like for you?

Sincerely,
Monse

"Netflix is life, to be honest."

Dear Monse,

I haven't watched *The People v. O.J. Simpson*. Maybe I'll watch that later. Right now I'm watching *Shameless*. It's really good but inappropriate at times. One place that I want to travel to is obviously Belize because that's where I'm from and I have a lot of family there. Another place where I would like to travel is Hawaii because, living in Chicago, I would like to go someplace warm and relaxing.

High school, for me, was fun my freshman year, but it was also hard work. The best thing to do is just make a lot of friends and focus on your work. If you just do that you will be fine in high school, and it also helps to join sports or a club. When I get older there are two things that I would want as a career. The first thing is to become an NBA player, but I know how rare that is, so I would also like to be an electrical engineer.

This is my last letter so hopefully we'll get to meet in person at that summer book release. Good luck in high school.

Sincerely,
Kristian DeLao

KRISTIAN DELAO is a sixteen-year-old sophomore in Chicago at Amundsen High School. Kristian likes to play a lot of sports. He has been living in Chicago all his life. He is from Belize. He is a football and basketball player. He is smart and really good at math. His dreams are to be drafted into the NBA or to become an electrical engineer.

MONSERRAT GARCIA is a fourteen-year-old who will start off shy but become goofy. She is a total bookworm who will read 24/7 (or when she has time). She is from Chicago and lives in a great neighborhood called Little Village with lots of caring people and of Mexican culture. She hopes to grow up and be someone with a great future, maybe a chef.

TIC-TAC-WRITE

Just like in tic-tac-toe, choose three prompts in a row (move vertically, horizontally, or diagonally) and include your answers in your next letter.

What does *freedom* mean to you? Share a story of a time you felt free.	How is your parents' life different from yours? Would you want to switch places? Why or why not?	What is your first memory? How do you feel when you think of this memory?
Think of a place or person that is special to you. Describe your subject using all of your senses.	FREE SPACE! Write about whatever you want. What's on your mind might now?	Write about the best day of your life.
What does the word *hope* mean to you? Share a story of a time you felt either hope*ful* or hope*less*.	Tell the story of a time someone stole something from you.	Describe your neighborhood at 7 a.m. on a Sunday morning, or 7 p.m. on a Friday night.

"Peace out, and take care."

AREON WHITE & GUADALUPE GOMEZ

Dear Areon,

What's up? My name is Guadalupe, and yes, as you can tell by my name, I'm Mexican. I am just a simple thirteen-year-old girl who is five-foot-two. A short summary about me is that, once you get to know me, I am a very chill person. I have a big sense of humor to be honest, but there's a side of me that is very shy.

Some things I would like to know about you are: How old are you? What's your hobby? What are you studying? What was your freshman year like? What race are you? How tall are you? And simply, how ya' been? Sorry for a lot of questions, haha.

I guess you can say that we do have some things in common. For example, we are both looking forward to college. Then again, we are both worried that it might be too difficult. You also said that your biggest concern as an eighth grader was not being able to fit in and not feeling smart enough. I can also relate to that. Also, because I'm just in eighth grade right now, I honestly don't consider myself that smart. So, don't worry about it because you're not the only one.

Hopefully we can become cool with each other and maybe be friends. Peace out, Areon, and take care.

Sincerely,
Guadalupe Gomez

Dear Guadalupe,

My name is Areon White and I am fifteen years old. I'm African American. I am between five-foot-ten and five-foot-twelve. My hobbies are hanging out with friends and playing basketball, football, or video games. The things I do with my friends are go to the beach and play basketball. Being with friends can help you express yourself or help with being shy. Friends can help you out with lots of things such as relationships, grades, work, and your feelings.

I play lots of video games and am actually planning on making a YouTube channel about gaming. What games do you play?

About friends, don't get distracted and act up too much with them. I learned that the hard way.

Sincerely,
Areon White

Dear Areon,

From your recent letter, you seem like a pretty chill and active guy. You must really like playing video games too. What else are you interested in? And even though I am a girl, I play some video games here and there. Games like *Clash Royale*, *Call of Duty*, and *Grand Theft Auto V*. I can't say that I'm an expert at playing these games, but I'm all right.

About you wanting to make a YouTube channel, I think that you should just do it. If you think that you should make one, then go for it. Just make sure you have planned what you're going to make it about. Who is your favorite YouTuber? I really don't have a favorite YouTuber, but I really like Reaction Time. What content do you enjoy watching? Personally, I like funny Vines.

Have you ever had the best day of your life? I can't say that I have had one, but every year my family and I go to Mexico for the summer. We get to see our family over there and have lots of fun. We have a fire outside, ride motorcycles, and enjoy the nice weather. I ♥ going to Mexico.

What's on your mind right now? Like anything at all. I'm thinking about music and food. I haven't had McDonald's in a while and I ♥ music. What's your favorite food? Do you love music? That concludes this letter. Can't wait to hear back from you. Take care.

Sincerely,
Guadalupe

Dear Guadalupe,

The video games I play are *Call of Duty*, *Grand Theft Auto V*, *Fallout*, sports games, and also campaign missions. Tell me about *Clash Royale*. What is it about? I will make a YouTube in the summer when I'll have more time. I haven't had the best day of my life yet either, but one of my favorite memories is when my friends took me to the beach for my birthday. We had a lot of fun. They bought me cookies, but the seagulls stole them. We all went in the water for an hour or longer, and when we came back, the cookies were everywhere in pieces! The type of YouTube videos I watch are comedy, sports, and gaming. My favorite food is hot wings and nachos.

How have you been feeling lately? I've been having different feelings lately because my best friend broke up with his girlfriend who I'm also close friends with. So, everyday she asks me things about him and it's annoying, but I understand how she feels because I've been through that too. I want to help. He has moved on, but she hasn't. I don't usually show my feelings, but sometimes I want to yell and tell her to move on because he has—but she's feeling emotional and I don't want her to cry. Have you ever been in between one of your friend's problems? It's hard to help.

Sincerely,
Areon

Hey Areon,

Well, as you know, this is the last letter. For starters, the game *Clash Royale* is about battling worldwide against anyone else who has the game. When you win, you receive trophies. Not the best game ever, but it's all right I guess.

Your birthday at the beach sounds like fun. The part with the seagulls eating your cookies was really funny. Speaking of food, my favorite food would be things from McDonald's, especially the Frappés. I like nachos like you do too.

By now, I am not sure if you have solved the drama between you and your best friend's ex. Is it done? If you still have this problem going on, then you should know that you shouldn't be worried. This isn't your fault and it isn't going to last forever. Life has ups and downs. If I were your best friend's ex, then I would really try to move on.

About my life right now, it's not the best, but it's all right. I don't want to get too into the details.

One memory I would like to share with you would be when my best friend got herself a boyfriend and I was jealous. She would always be talking about him and I would be like the third wheel. I would be home watching Netflix, and my best friend would text me asking if she and her boyfriend could come to my house. Since I had to sleep in the same room as my little sister, they would be on my sister's bed hanging out. I would be on my bed alone, watching them with death eyes while they hugged. I mean the guy is loyal and everything, and so is my friend, but they are both too attached. I'm afraid that they will get their hearts broken. I love them both because they are my best friends, and I want to see them happy.

Sincerely,
Guadalupe ♥

Hey Guadalupe,

I might try that *Clash Royale* game out—it sounds okay. I also like McDonald's but mostly their fries. I go all the time. And man, I love nachos. I could eat them every day. Me and my best friend's ex did finally make up, and she's trying to move on. It's hard for her, but I'm helping.

I understand that you don't wanna talk about your life, so I won't ask about it. Remember the things I told you about high school. Never let things get to you and distract you from learning or getting to school on time. High school is a big challenge. You'll have homework almost every day, and you should try your hardest in school all the time.

Sincerely,
Areon

P.S. My teacher just told me she thinks McDonald's fries are the bomb! LOL.

Hey Guadalope

I might try that game out, it sounds ok. Also my birthday was fun, it had some ups and down but it was fun. I also like mcdonalds but mostly their fries, I go almost all the time. Yes lol, I love nachos, I can eat them everyday. Me and my bestfriends made up and she's trying to move on but it's hard for her, but I'm helping. I understand that you don't wanna talk about your life, I won't ask about it. My friend Sam is going threw that with our friend bry but it's worse because the boyfriend is a twin, and her ex that she don't go with anymore is the twin brother so she's having a hard time. Also remember the things I told you about high school, never let things get to you and distract you from learning or getting to school on time. High school is a big challenge, you'll have homework almost everyday and you should try your hardest in school all the time.

Sincerely
Arion

P.S me and my teacher thinks mcdonald's fries are the bomb! LOL

AREON WHITE is a fifteen-year-old African American who plays basketball and football. Areon wants to be a basketball player or join the military to save our country.

GUADALUPE GOMEZ is a thirteen-year-old kid who lives in Chicago and loves watching Netflix while eating McDonald's. She sometimes gets overwhelmed by life, but she still tries to make the best of it. She hopes to attend a Justin Bieber concert when she grows up. She also wants to be like Salice Rose and Victor Ramon Perez (XVX.98), who are some of the funniest people she cannot see face-to-face. She wishes to meet them one day.

KUNJAME KHORN + ISAIAH JOHNSON & LUIS MUÑIZ

Dear Kunjame and Isaiah,

My name is Luis and I am thirteen years old. My favorite TV show is *The Big Bang Theory* and my favorite character is Sheldon Cooper. I like video games and I own a PS4. My favorite game so far is *Modern Warfare Remastered*. Do you like video games? If so, what console and what's your favorite game? What's your TV show?

I like to read any type of book as long as it is not nonfiction. My favorite author is Rick Riordan. I guess that we do have something in common. Books have always been an important part of my life in moments when I have been alone. They never let me down.

To start off, do you guys have girlfriends? I know it's an awkward question, but I really want to know. What is your favorite music, band, or singer? My favorite band is Twenty One Pilots, and I like all of their songs except "The Judge." What's your favorite food? I like *tortas*. What ethnicity are you? Tell me more about your hobbies or lives.

Sincerely,
Luis M.

Dear Luis,

Here is some information on me, Kunjame. I am of Asian descent. I was born and raised in Cambodia. This is a small little country in the southern-east part of Asia. Until I was four years old, I struggled with my family in our hometown, Phnom Penh. This is the capital. Growing up was tough because I wasn't rich but neither was I poor. I was the only child until my brother was born, two years later. And later my other siblings were born, two years after each other. Now my mom has three other kids to care for.

On my fourth birthday, my family and I moved to the U.S. to find a better place to live, and so my parents could get jobs. Moving to a new country foreign to my own was strange. They spoke words of a different tongue. I would walk in the streets wondering what they were saying.

Now you know a bit about my life and its origins, so I would like to know about yours, if you may share. To answer your question, no, I am not in a relationship, mainly because I feel as if people would get hurt.

I was also wondering if you enjoy any music that isn't in English? If so, can you tell me about those musicians? I am running out of things to say or ask. I hope we can learn more about each other.

Your new friend,
Kunjame or "James"

Dear Luis,

I'm sorry I couldn't write back to you on time. Here are some questions I want to ask you:

1. What do you like to do for fun?
2. Do you have a boyfriend or a girlfriend?
3. How old are you?
4. What school are you going to next year?

Here is stuff about me: I love to play video games. I have four sisters and three brothers. I'm the oldest. I'm seventeen years old. I love to play basketball and soccer. I have a girlfriend. I love to play cards. I hate cartoons. That's all.

Sincerely,
Isaiah Johnson

Dear Kunjame and Isaiah,

To answer your first question, my parents are from Mexico and they met in a restaurant here in Chicago. They took time to meet each other and then had my sister. Two years later, they had me. Now I'm thirteen years old and I'm turning fourteen on April 1. I'm not kidding.

To answer your other question, I listen to Korean music. My sister makes me listen to it. What are your favorite types of music, games, and TV shows? Mine is *The Big Bang Theory* and my favorite character is Howard Wolowitz. What was your favorite Christmas? Mine was when I got a package and I opened it up early even though I wasn't supposed to.

What do you wanna be when you grow up? I wanna to be a computer engineer or a graphic designer. I would like to hear back from you.

TTYL,
Luis Muñiz

Dear Luis,

I'm about to answer your questions.

Q: What is your favorite type of music?
A: My favorite type of music is rap. My favorite rapper is Tupac. Tupac is my favorite rapper because he has the best poems ever.

Q: What is your favorite movie?
A: My favorite movie is *The Brothers Grimsby*. It's my favorite movie because it's the funniest movie ever.

Q: What is your favorite TV show?
A: My favorite TV show is *Third Watch*. It's about a cop who does crime.

Q: When was your favorite Christmas?
A: My favorite Christmas was when I got a puppy.

Q: What do you want to be when you grow up?
A: I want to be a lawyer when I grow up.

Story time! It starts out with how I went on a trip to the Shedd Aquarium. It was a midsummer day and my mom told me that we were going. I got to pet the stingrays. They were so cool. It was the best day ever!

Sincerely,
Isaiah

Dear Luis,

I'm about to answer questions.

Q: What is your favorite type of music?

A: My favorite type of music is rap. My favorite rapper is Tupac. Tupac is my favorite rapper because he does the best poems ever.

Q: What is your movie?

A: My favorite movie is The Grembsy family. It's my favorite movie because it's the funniest movie ever.

Q: What is your favorite T.V. show?

A: My favorite TV show is "Third Watch". It's about a cop who does crime.

Q: When was your favorite Christmas?

A: My favorite Christmas is when I got a puppy. I got the puppy when I was 12.

"I woke up on Christmas morning to some very obnoxious caroling."

Dear Luis,

I am a diehard fan of K-pop and I love how your sister opened you up to it. It needs more appreciation. When we meet in person, I will tell you more. I do not really have a favorite American TV show. I am more into anime and drama. They're more of a sufficient time-waster for me. Most of my favorite comedies cannot be watched online, at least not legally. Knowing that this is the last letter pre-meetup, I will share a story.

I have a present that I cling to so much from a Christmas long ago, back when I was in eighth grade. I woke up on Christmas morning to some very obnoxious caroling, but I went back to sleep until 2 p.m. A while later it was time to dine, but I just stared out the window to an abyss of nothingness. Why? Because I was baffled that it wasn't a white Christmas. I sighed faintly and mumbled to myself, "What is this crap?"

Little did I know, all of my relatives were partying downstairs whilst I sat depressed contemplating life. My eyes slowly closed and the next thing I heard was "James, wake up! Time to get your present!" I flew out of bed and ran out of my room, sliding around corners and bolting down the corridor to the living room. To my surprise, I saw a small package. I was anxious as everyone in my general vicinity took pictures of me opening my gift. It was a shirt! I liked how the green contrasts highly with the black outlining right away. It was a sight to see. It said the giver was anonymous, but I know it was, of course, my older cousin. From then on I've always either worn this shirt or kept it as a prized possession in my closet. This is a favorite memory of mine.

Until we meet,
Kunjame Khorn

KUNJAME KHORN is a pop music and dance enthusiast. He loves math and hates desserts that are too sweet. He specializes in a plethora of music genres and martial arts. As a child he enjoyed theatre and acting in general. He was also very ignorant and not the nicest. Teachers always butcher his name in the funkiest ways—it goes from Konami to Kunyame. When he is an adult, his dream job will be a software engineer or music dance leader.

ISAIAH JOHNSON loves to play sports and lives in Chicago. He wants to be a lawyer or forensic person when he grows up. He has nine sisters and three brothers. He is the oldest. He goes to Amundsen High School. He's a rapper, a singer, and a pianist. He's a dancer. He's in tenth grade.

LUIS ALBERTO MUÑIZ, age fourteen, is addicted to video games. Give him a new video game and he can complete it in a week. He also questions a lot of things. He questions what's the meaning of life and why we are here. He has a weird laugh that he does not like at all. He wants to be a graphic designer.

The brain works in mysterious ways. Pick a random word below and see how it jogs your memory. What stories come to the surface? Share one of these memories in your next letter.

VANILLA

SIREN

CAR

ROBOT

PORCH

UNUSUAL

LOCK

FORTUNE

STAR

BIRD

BRADY MATTESON & JEFFREY CORREA

Dear Brady Matteson,

Do you listen to Jon Bellion? Some good songs are "Jim Morrison," "All Time Low," and "Wonder Years." What type of YouTube videos do you want to make? Do you play *Clash Royale*? If you do, tell me more about your account. I am almost a Level Eight. I can't wait to be a Level Eight, because then I can go to tournaments and get some more cards.

Wow, I just noticed I did not say my name is Jeffrey, but you can call me Jeff. I was a shy person, but not anymore.

From,
Jeffrey Correa

Dear Jeff,

I don't know who Jon Bellion is. I do listen to all the bands listed on the back of this letter, though. I recommend you check some of them out. I got into them through my dad, the internet, and my friends. My YouTube channel started after I watched some old Lego animation and I thought, *Hey, I can do that too!* The channel has vlogs, animation, comedy, music, tutorials, etc. I'm not much of a gamer. I love horror movies and drawing. My questions are: what do you expect out of high school and what do you think it will be like?

Thanks,
Brady Matteson

Dear Brady Matteson,

Thank you for the letter. One of the bands that you listed, I know: Twenty One Pilots. I have heard the music that they make and it is good. I have asked my classmates if they know who Jon Bellion. They said no. He is really good, though. I would give Jon Bellion a five-star rating on most of his songs. For Twenty One Pilots, I don't know most of their songs. I stopped listening to Twenty One Pilots years ago.

I think that my favorite day of my life was when I got my dog Butters. Her full name is Butterscotch. (My sister named her.) My cousins had a big black dog called Knight. He was a good dog and everyone loved him. He loved everyone, but he died of cancer. My dog is small, but even though she is small, she jumps high.

What is your favorite day of your life and why?

From,
Jeffrey

"I have two goals for the show. One is to be in the front row and the other is to catch a drumstick at the end."

Dear Jeffrey,

I'm sorry to hear about your dog. I've got three of my own—they're all pretty old. One is sixteen, another is ten, and the youngest is six. The oldest is a black lab and the other two are mini dachshunds.

To answer your question, I would say the best day of my life was getting to go to a music festival called Mayhem Fest to see two of my favorite bands, Mastodon and Slipknot. I was seven when I saw them. After the show, I got to meet Mastodon at a free meet and greet! My dad, my brother, and I were in line, and they were about to start heading out for their next gig. I don't exactly remember who it was that called us up—it was either the drummer or the bassist. They signed posters and magazines for us, and they were very nice!

I haven't gotten to see them live since. Fortunately, they recently announced a new album and tour! I'm going to see them at the Aragon Ballroom in May. I'm super hyped to see them, especially since the drummer, Brann Dailor, is my idol. I have two goals for the show. One is to be in the front row and the other is to catch a drumstick at the end of the show. The drummer usually sticks around after they finish their show to throw shirts and drumsticks into the crowd.

Personally, Mastodon holds a special place in my heart. They were the first real metal band I ever saw live. They had a much larger influence on my drumming and my love for music in general, much more than Slipknot ever could. That, and Mastodon hasn't ever had a bad album. Their style of music puts me in a *zone* sort of state. It's hard to describe. They're an incredible band in the studio and live. It's weird—I've only seen them once, but I've listened to them my whole life and they're such an influence on me.

Who inspires you? Let me know!

Sincerely,
Brady Matteson

Dear Brady,

Wow, this is the last letter that I will be sending—time flies by really fast. The school year is almost over. The good thing is that I have my friends and classmates on social media so we can all talk and have fun.

I would tell you that you should appreciate the things that you have right now. When I got into my bike accident, I was not able to use my right hand and the things that were easy were hard. We all take stuff for granted. Just because we have someone or something does not mean that we will have it forever.

Currently, I am working on making my own PC and this PC is going to be one of the best. I might get an i5 core processor instead of an i7. Making my own PC would be better, so I can overclock it to make it better. I have never made a PC before, so it will be my first time. I think I know what to do. I might make a video on it. How do you feel about the Samsung S8? It might be better than the iPhone.

From,
Jeffrey Correa

Dear Brady

wow this is the last letter that I will be sending, time flies by really fast. The school year is almost over. The good thing is that I have my friends and classmates on social media so we can all talk and have fun. My dog is really nice and is better, so I am happy about that. My brother comes home only a few times a month.

I would tell you that you should appreciate the things that you have right now. When I got in to my bike accident I was not able to use my right hand so the things that were easy were hard. We all take stuff for granted just because we have someone or something does not mean that we will have it forever.

So currently I am working on making my own PC, and this PC is going to be one of the best. I might get an i5 core prosesor not an i7. Making my own PC would be better, since I can put what I need. I can everclock it to make it better.

I have never made a PC before, so it will be my first time. I think I know what to do. I might make a video on it. How do you feel about the Samsung S8 it might be better than the iphone.

from,
Jeffrey Correa

Dear Jeffrey,

You're telling me! I'm halfway to graduating from high school. It's crazy how fast it goes by. That's a shame to hear about your arm—I just got over being sick. I remember breaking my arm on Halloween in second grade. I fell off a log while trying to save a bag of candy. I couldn't trick-or-treat that night.

It's really cool to hear that you're working on building a PC. I've never tried it before. I've been getting more into coding and programming computers. I've been taking a class in programming and coding at Amundsen for a few months now, and I've even built a working website!

I have a bit of advice for when you get to high school: it's nothing like the movies. It's nothing to seriously worry about. You'll be fine as long as you have good time management.

Sincerely,
Brady Matteson

BRADY MATTESON is a fifteen-year-old sophomore at Amundsen High School. He listens to the Deftones, Mastodon, and the Death Grips. He plays the drums. He loves instant photography and his prized Polaroid camera. At his first concert, he saw and met Mastodon at Mayhem Fest '08. That was pretty cool.

JEFFREY CORREA is an eighth grader at Zapata Academy. He has a YouTube channel where he makes videos about games like *Clash Royale*. He is working on a song to release that he has been working on for some time. He likes to ride his bike and have fun with friends. He also likes to play different sports. He is working on becoming stronger physically. He is a good friend and a good brother. He was a shy person. He used to be a lazy person, but now he wants to become stronger and a better song producer. He also thinks about others. He can't help but help when others need help.

"You're probably gonna think I'm weird, but what type of shoes do you wear?"

REUBEN RILEY & GISELLE CARDOZA

Dear Reuben Riley,

To begin with, my name is Giselle Cardoza Villanueva. I'm fourteen years old. I was born on September 19, 2002 in Chicago. I'm Mexican American and both my parents are Mexican. Therefore, I speak English and Spanish. I have seven siblings, and with me, we're eight. Only three of us are here and the rest are in Mexico. How many siblings do you have?

I listen to *banda*, trap rap, *bachata*, and a little of *musica urbana*. My favorite singers are Drake, Kodak Black, Maluma, Romeo Santos, Future, Cluco, Banda MS, and Ariel Camacho. I play basketball, and I have practice on Tuesday and Thursday. I like trying new things, making people laugh, having fun, and partying a lot with my friends. I love food! The type of food I like is Mexican food. It's the best.

But enough about me. I would like to know, how was the beginning of your freshman year? Do you play any sports? If so, which one? What sport do you hate? How old are you? When's your birthday? What type of music do you like? Can you describe yourself using five words?

What is the first memory you ever had? The first thing I remember remembering is my friend Jasmin. She died when I was in sixth grade. Today would actually be her birthday, December 20, 2016. How I feel about this is sad because I really miss her a lot.

You're probably gonna think I'm weird, but what type of shoes do you wear? I hope you can answer all of my questions. I hope we can get to know each other more! I guess that's it.

Sincerely,
Giselle Cardoza

Dear Giselle,

Hello, my name is Reuben. I'm African American and I play basketball. I'm really talented and I play JV, also known as Junior Varsity. The position I play is shooting guard, which also known as the 2. I like to play video games like *AK*, *Call of Duty*, *GTA*, and *Madden*. I play on PS4. My favorite food is Hispanic food because I grew up around a lot of Hispanic people. They lived in my neighborhood and they were my really close friends, basically my family. I enjoy being around friends. Whether we're just hanging out or playing basketball, I love being with my bros.

What does freedom mean to me? Freedom to me was the day I got my cast off after I sprained my arm. When I was in camp, when I was younger, we were playing on the monkey bars in the park. We were unsupervised because our camp leaders weren't watching, so I was jumping to all of the bars and I slipped because the bar was wet. I fell and sprained my arm, but I didn't tell anyone. When I got home from camp, I told my dad. He was upset and mad that I hadn't told anyone. So, we iced it for a while and used Icy Hot packs. We used the whole box.

The next day, we went to St. Francis Hospital to get x-rayed and have my arm checked out. They brought me into the room and x-rayed my arm from all different angles. We found out what was wrong and it was a sprained arm. I had to wear this cast for about six months. I was upset because this cast held me back from activities and sports that I would've liked to play. So, time went by and the day finally came when I could finally get this cast off. After he took it off, the doctor told me to keep exercising so it could get back to full strength. He recommended swimming, and once we left the facility I went straight to the beach. I was very happy and glad that I got it taken off.

Peace out,
Reuben

Dear Reuben,

Hey boi, wassup! You sound like a very fun and interesting person. Thank you for sharing that amazing letter with me. The story you told me was amazing! I really appreciate it. I feel bad for you having that cast on for so long. I would have gotten stressed and taken it off. I'm glad that you're okay now, but if you're in a camp, aren't you supposed to supervised 24/7?

There was this one time when I fell down the stairs and I didn't tell anyone either. That day I had a modeling casting and my heel fell off. I fell all the way to the bottom of the stairs then got up like nothing happened. Everyone came rushing, but I just played it off like I was fine.

I'm looking forward to meeting you in person soon. It was nice meeting you through these letters.

Giselle Cardoza Villanueva

P.S. Can you give me some tips for basketball?

Dear Giselle,

Thank you for liking my story. I really appreciate it. Yes, camp supervisors are supposed to watch us, but at the time they were just talking to one another and had their backs turned away from us. Yeah, that's what happened.

I have questions about your modeling casting. First off, I hope that when you fell you didn't hurt anything and that your modeling stuff continues to go well. Also, how did you fall down the stairs that day? Did you trip? Were you coming up or down from the stairs when you fell?

Is modeling what you to do for life? I know what I want in life is to be successful in my education, in basketball, and in my whole life. It'll for sure be a challenge, but I know for a fact that I'm up for it. I'm proud to be working hard to achieve my goals and staying focused.

Looking forward to seeing you soon.

Yours truly,
Reuben Riley

REUBEN RILEY is an African American male who is talented at basketball. His dreams and hopes are to be in the NBA. He knows that it will be hard, but he also knows that he can achieve it by working hard and staying focused. He wishes to be successful, fulfill his dreams, and make his family proud.

GISELLE CARDOZA VILLANUEVA is a fourteen-year-old who lives in Chicago and attends eighth grade at Emiliano Zapata Academy. She enjoys eating, cleaning, and sleeping. She loves Mexican food. She's from Durango and Zacatecas. She wishes to travel the world. Giselle enjoys modeling, shopping, and makeup. She is a purple belt in Taekwondo and would love to attempt boxing. She loves to party and dance to *norteñas*, *corridos*, *huapangos*, *cumbia*, and *zapatiados*. When she is older, she would like to live in Durango. She wants to be a lawyer and a successful person.

ANAHI FERRER & MIA GUEVARA

Dear Anahi,

Hey! I'm Mia—get ready—Mia Simone Guevara Villalobos Imperial. Yeah. That's my name. Long story short, my mom and my father, Joe, separated. Then my mom married Walter, my new dad, when I was just five years old. Yeah, my dad was technically my stepdad, but Walter stepped up and was more of a dad than my father will EVER be. I lost him this year in December. I guess I only had a dad long enough to teach me how to love and to learn my rights and wrongs.

I miss him so much, but I know he's my guardian angel now and he's not suffering anymore. I only had him for a little while, but it was the best time of my life and always will be, to be honest.

So, I will start you off with a bio of myself: I am a thirteen-year-old Mexican-Honduran-Puerto Rican living in a Hispanic neighborhood, Little Village. I'm such a city girl. I love Chicago! I wouldn't trade it for anywhere else in the world. My favorite colors? Pink, maroon, and black. I love shoes! I'm deeply in love with The Weeknd, Drake, and Kodak Black. Oh, and I can't forget Montana 300. Music is a big part of my life. I'm in the All-City Chorus and have already done six solos. I've been there for three years, but I've been in choir since I was seven years old.

I usually spend my time on homework or with my boyfriend, Andres. I also spend time on volleyball, on basketball, and with my mom. Well, how about you, Anahi? Can you relate to anything I wrote, or am I your total opposite? I wanna know if we really do connect like I think we do. LOL.

I'ma ask you a few quick questions. How was your freshman year? What's your main goal in life? What's your boyfriend like? Any advice to give me? What colleges are you thinking about? Any more questions for me? Well, see ya soon, girl!

♥ ♥ ♥ ♥ ♥

Sincerely,
Mia Guevara
♥ ♥ ♥

P.S. I'll tell you more later! ♥ XOXO

"I dress depending on my mood, but the color I wear most is black. Don't think I'm emo though. I just like dark colors."

Dear Mia,

Hey girl! How are you? :) As you know, my name is Anahi Ferrer. I'm in tenth grade at Amundsen High School. I have a big family. I'm the seventh child out of nine. It's the worst to be the youngest because you argue a lot and get blamed for a lot of childish things.

Anyway, I'm on an indoor soccer team and I'm still waiting for my soccer season to start here at Amundsen. I started in seventh grade and have loved it ever since. When I play soccer I don't care if they put me as forward, midfield, defense, or goalie. I can play in every position. Dance is my thing too.

I dress depending on my mood, but the color I wear most is black. Don't think I'm emo though. I just like dark colors. I'm a really sensitive person and I care about other people.

So, I heard you have a boyfriend. How long you been with him? Is he treating you right? HE BETTER! LOL. I can't wait to meet you. See you soon!

Sincerely,
Anahi Ferrer

Dear Anahi,

Hey girl! ♥ As you know, we are working on the Tic-Tac-Write assignment. I chose the first box and then went down vertically because I felt that, with those, my true feelings and personality would come out to you ♥. Feel me?

Okay, first things first: *what does freedom mean to you? Tell a story of a moment when you felt free.* Okay, *freedom* to me means power, strength, and courage—the happiness with being able to make your own choices, no matter what ♥. A moment when I feel free is when I'm home alone or when I'm out somewhere without adults. This is because being home alone is great. You feel relaxed and worry-free.

Second question: *Think of a place or person that is special to you. Describe your subject using all of your senses.* My favorite people are ♥ Andres ♥ and ♥ my mom ♥. Andres makes me feel comfortable, trustworthy, safe, protected, and loved. He helps me see the good times and makes me remember them all because they are ALWAYS great memories ♥. When I think about him, I hear music or his sweet words, sometimes even advice ♥. I always smell his cologne and it smells so, so, so good! Honestly, I'm tasting food: chips and candy ♥.

With my mom, I hear advice and sometimes yelling, LOL, and her saying "I love you" everyday. I feel warm, comfortable, sort of like a baby when I'm with her, LOL. I see TV or memories that are happening, like long drives, going out to eat, and much more. I smell her Carmex chapstick and Eternity perfume mixed up together. I taste gum or home cooked meals ♥.

My favorite place is Six Flags because it makes me feel really energized, excited, and happy. I smell fresh air and water park chlorine water. I taste junk food ♥. Yum, LOL ♥. I hear lots of screams and see my family together as we should always be (yet aren't). Lastly I see my beautiful family, smiles, fun experiences, and amazing memories ♥.

My last question is *what does the word hope mean to you? Have you ever felt hopeful or hopeless? Write about that time.* The word *hope* to me is honestly just a word. *Hope* to me is just an addition to the dictionaries. Now, let me tell you why I believe this. My dad would always tell me that you must work for everything you receive. Simply hoping something will happen won't get you anywhere. My dad was desperate to stick by my side and be there for me as he was getting sicker. So, he hoped and prayed he'd get better, yet that got him nowhere. He *hoped*, but I guess it just wasn't good enough.

Sincerely,
Mia Guevara

Dear Anahi,

Hey boo! ♥ I've been really good. To be honest, a lil' stressed and tired from school and sports, but I got this, LOL. I see you're not so good, mama ♥. I hope you receive none but the best, and may God bless you 'cause you're a blessing. Don't let anyone make you feel any less, beautiful. I get that guys are tryin' to get at yo' cute self. I mean, talk to a few. One could be your soul mate, LOL! ♥ I also get that people can be hella childish and don't wanna see you make it in a strong and happy relationship. Girl, forget them and NEVER CHASE A BOY! If Eduardo loves or cares for you like you think he does, he'll run back to you, girly ♥.

Being in a relationship is amazing and comforting. Me and my boyfriend have been together currently two years and two months, and we've never been better. Our bond is unbreakable. Haters hate and try very hard to see us apart, but they can't! They're just unhappy, ignorant people who wish they had what I have. Yet lemme be honest, if you've been through a few relationships and they haven't worked out, don't you think you should give it a lil' break for a while? Try the single life ♥. Join an activity, sport, club, etc. Try to get honor roll, better yourself, start thinking about your future and how you're going to make money rather than who you're gonna be with, baby girl ♥. You gotta love yourself before you love someone else. Follow your heart AND your head, boo ♥. Don't let NO ONE bring you down or interfere with your decisions. Well, there's my advice, take it or leave it ♥.

On a totally different note, here's a super creepy and sad story from when I went to visit my dad's grave on Christmas Eve. My grandma and grandpa (my dad's parents), pulled up in front of my big pink house in their white Volvo. We got in and rushed to pick up my boyfriend Andres because we were running kind of late. About half an hour later, we were across the street from the cemetery in a flower shop that sells many, many things for graves. We walked in to get one of those bouquets that you can place into the ground of the grave. We picked one that's green and black roses. As we were walking out, the flower shop lady stopped my mom and me, and she gave my mom a rosary—it was royal blue, my mom's favorite color in the whole universe. The words that came out of the lady's mouth send chills up my spine just thinking about them. She said, "Your husband been wanting you to have this. It's on the house."

By the way, this was our first time going to the shop. Considering the fact my dad had passed away, it was impossible for this to happen, right? My mom broke out crying, but forced out a thank you. She told me to grab the bouquet and meet her in the car. I was at the edge of crying too, but I didn't because I hate crying in front of people. I turned to the lady—her name tag read Sara. She handed me the bouquet and said, "Stop holding it in. If you hold it in too long you'll explode. Your dad says to let go. He's okay and watching over you. He never forgets to give you butterfly kisses."

I was speechless. I ran out of there with tears coming down my face one hundred miles an hour. To this day I cannot get Sara's voice out of my head. How could this woman know so much about my family? The comfort she gave was perfect, and she released all the stress I was holding onto so tightly in just a matter of minutes. In case you don't know what butterfly kisses are, it's when someone blinks their eyelashes across your cheek. My dad did it to me EVERY NIGHT, no matter how old I got.

I miss him so much, and no matter what I do I cannot bring him back :(. What really hurts is I won't have a father-daughter dance at my Quinceañera. He won't be there to see his daughters' high school graduations, he won't be there to walk me down the aisle at my wedding, and he won't be there for his grandchildren someday. My dad was my life and my life was taken from me too soon.

Well, this is our last letter session. Can't wait to meet you girl! Sorry to leave on a sad note. I wanted to share something really deep. Hoping you do the same ♥. I love you ♥. See ya in June ♥.

Love,
Ya favorite girl, Mia G.

ANAHI FERRER is a sophomore who attends Amundsen High School. A sixteen-year-old girl who cares about others and herself, she's a friend, a daughter, a sister. She enjoys playing soccer, singing, and dancing. You can open up to her whenever you need someone to talk to. Just know she's always there.

MIA S. GUEVARA is a proud, confident teenager from the city she adores: Chicago. She is determined to pursue every single dream she desires. She is strong and will never look back to that rotten rebel she used to be. She's in love with OVOXO ♥. Her heart and soul craves a music career, yet her mind is heading toward joining her family's generations of doctors ♥. **P.S.** Don't catch her in the morning, she's kind of a grinch. LOL.

LOVE LETTER TO MYSELF

3 THINGS I LIKE ABOUT MYSELF:

_____
_____
_____

3 THINGS I LOVE TO DO:

_____
_____
_____

3 THINGS I'LL DO TO CELEBRATE MYSELF <u>TODAY</u>:

_____
_____
_____

NOW WRITE YOURSELF
A LOVE LETTER:

Dear Me,

RAMÓN OCEGUEDA & BALTAZAR CAMARENA

Dear Ramón Ocegueda,

Hi, my name is Baltazar Camarena. My name is weird so my friends call me Balta. You can call me Balta too. I have two brothers and I'm the oldest. I like to play soccer. My favorite class is gym and dismissal time.

I like to listen to Mexican music when I'm bored, or play video games. Especially *Grand Theft Auto V* or *FIFA 17*. I also like to go into my phone to use Facebook or Snapchat, or watch YouTube videos and Netflix. My favorite show is one called *Los Heroes del Norte*. It is in Spanish. I like it because it's so funny. I also like *El Señor de los Cielos* and *El Chema*.

In my class, we are learning about life lessons. Have you ever learned one? I have. One time I was running in the house and I broke my finger. I had to have surgery.

The first thing I remember from when I was little is when I got my first pet. He is a dog named Bingo. He means a lot to me. He has been there since I was little. He follows me everywhere. I still have him, but now he's in Mexico with my grandparents. Last summer, I went to Mexico. I got to see Bingo and my grandparents.

My favorite person is my favorite cousin because he is always there for me. We always play video games. At the family parties, we don't get bored because we're there together.

Do you have a favorite person? How old are you? Are you Latino? What songs do you like? Do you like soccer or other sports? I can't wait to read your letter.

Sincerely,
Baltazar Camarena

Dear Balta,

Hi, my name is Ramón Ocegueda and I'm fifteen. I am Latino and was born in Mexico. I'm from El Carmen, Jalisco. I haven't lived there for a long time, but my dad said that when we're done building the house we're building, we're going to move there forever. I want to go because it's more calm over there. You don't have to worry about nothing. I have a lot of friends over there. My best friend over there is Toño. We've been friends since day one. We used to play a lot of soccer and we used to work together. People would send us to do *mandados* and we would get paid sometimes.

I like soccer and sometimes play in the street with my friends. My favorite team is Las Chivas. I watch whenever they play against América. I don't really like other sports, but I do like the White Sox because they're on the South Side. I don't like the Cubs. I don't got brothers, only a sister. I like to play video games too. I like any type of song, but I listen to *narcocorridos* the most.

Do you like school? To be honest, I don't. If I had an option to go to work or school, I would go to work. How's eighth grade? Do you like Trump?

Sincerely,
Ramón Ocegueda

Dear Ramón,

I'm from Mexico like you! I'm from a place called Culiacán, Sinaloa. I can see we like the same kind of music. Next time, can you recommend some good songs that you like? My favorite artist is a group called Grupo Fernandez and Revolver Cannabis. You should listen to those groups.

Eighth grade is going well and I'm doing good except in science. I always get bad grades in science, but the good thing is that I'm doing well in math and reading. Those are the grades that count. Tuesday is my favorite day of school because, in the first period, 826CHI comes. Also, that day we have gym. Which one is your favorite class? Which is your favorite day of school?

You asked if I like Trump. I don't because he does not like Mexicans and all of my family is Mexican, but they do have papers. Why do you want to go to Mexico? Aren't you going to miss it here? I went to Jalisco like two times. It's cool. I went to Guadalajara. Have you been to Guadalajara? As you know, I'm from Culiacán, Sinaloa. It's cool there. I have friends there. There's this girl named Wendy and she is also from Culiacán. We like the same music and she is cool. She is my friend, but when I moved to Chicago, she moved to León Guanajuato. We still talk on Facebook.

There's also this friend called Rafael Gomez. I call him Rafa. He sings in Grupo Rebeldia. Check him out on YouTube.

I'm going to tell you about when I first got here to Zapata. It was in fifth grade. The first days were hard because when you are a new kid you don't know no one. My first friends were Santiago and Joshua. Then, I started talking to Jorge. He is now my best friend. He has been in the same homeroom in fifth, sixth, seventh, and now eighth grade!

I don't know what else to say or write, so bye and take care.

Sincerely,

Balta

> Dear Balta,
>
> This the last letter and I just wanted to tell you that it was nice knowing you. You seem like a nice person but you should bring your science grade up. It couts too I did the same thing and when I got here I didt know how to do nothing. I've been to Guadalajara it looks like an ugly 26th street but la plaza looks cool and funcy my whole family is mexican too but not a lot have papers I have a lot of friends from when I was little that still friends with but some have died R.I.R Antonio he was my friend since day one we usto alwais chill together have a nice life
>
> Sinlerely Ramon Ozguedn

Dear Balta,

This is the last letter and I just wanted to tell you that it was nice knowing you. You seem like a nice person, but you should bring your science grade up. It counts too. I did the same thing because when I got here I didn't know how to do anything.

I've been to Guadalajara and it looks like an ugly 26th street. But *la plaza* looks cool and fancy. My whole family is Mexican too but not a lot have papers. I have a lot of friends from when I was little who I'm still friends with, but some have died. RIP Antonio, he was my friend since day one. We used to always chill together.

Have a nice life.

Sincerely,
Ramón Ocegueda

RAMÓN OCEGUEDA is a sixteen-year-old from Chicago. He's been to Mexico and has an older sister. He spends a lot of time on the street because he lives far from school and he sometimes goes to chill outside with his friends. He doesn't have a favorite class because he doesn't like school because it's boring.

BALTAZAR CAMARENA is thirteen years old and likes people to call him Balta. He is from Culiacán, Sinaloa and he currently lives in Chicago. He might not be smart, but he is a good person and likes to make his friends laugh. He loves to eat tacos. He might be odd, but he likes to watch WWE wrestling and is a gamer. He likes to hang out with friends and would like to be a soccer player. He might not be the best, but he would try hard. He likes to be on his phone all day on Facebook, Snapchat, and Instagram. He likes to hang out with his cousin Fernando. He often wears a hoodie, Nike or Adidas pants, or jeans.

"Did you have a good New Year? I know mine was lit and I left all my problems in 2016."

CHRISTIAN QUEVEDO & ROMAN RAMIREZ

Dear Christian,

Hi, my name is Roman. I was born in Chicago and I go to Zapata Academy. Something about me is that I am not the only child. I have four other siblings. I am not confident in myself when it comes to math, even though people say I am one of the best at it. I do okay in school, but I am more like an athletic kid. I play football and I made it to the championships, but we took second place. I was sad, but whatever. I still made it to the finals and I'm proud of myself.

I like to play video games like *Grand Theft Auto V*. How about you? Some other things I would want to know are: do you play sports, and what's your favorite subject in school? Are you doing well in school? Where were you born? Did you have a good New Year? I know mine was lit and I left all my problems in 2016.

Sincerely,
Roman Ramirez #23

Dear Roman,

Thanks for that info you gave me. I got to know you just a little bit more. Now, here's a bit more info about me. I was born in Chicago in Uptown. I'm into video games and I like going outside from time to time. I like to play sports such as basketball, volleyball, tennis, and soccer. My favorite subject is PE. I'm doing all right in school.

I want to further address the topic of video games. I like to play video games because it's a way to escape reality and do things you can't do in real life. The type of video games I like to play are RPGs (Role Playing Games) and action games. I don't really like to play on a console, just on a PC.

Question time! I only have one and that is: what's the funniest thing that has ever happened in school? That's all, see you next time! Thanks for reading.

Sincerely,
Christian Q.

P.S. What does the #23 on the back of your letter mean? Sorry I don't know :).

Wassup Christian,

Man, today is Valentine's Day. I forgot to tell you, but I got a girl and her name is Paola. I've been with her since October 24, 2016. For today, I bought her a teddy bear. Not one of those little ones but one of the BIG ones that's about three or four feet tall with a big purse that had all this little girly stuff in there. It was a red bag with a balloon attached to it. Hope you have a good day today!

Sincerely,
Roman #23

Dear Roman,

Today I'm going to write to you about how I practice dodging bullets on a day-to-day basis in my neighborhood. I live in the heart of Uptown and many people shoot, so sometimes it's like playing a survival game. It's not like they shoot every single day, but it happens.

One time I was at work—I'm a cashier—and there was this loud boom. I thought it was a firecracker, but I went outside to see nothing there. Later, the police showed up and I found out it was a driveby. Keep in mind the boom was right behind me.

Okay, that's as much as I could write. I only have four minutes. I'm writing this on March 7, 2017. Can't wait to see you in real life =D.

Sincerely,
Christian Q.

CHRISTIAN QUEVEDO isn't your ordinary teen! Oh no! This is a teen with a personality so weird, you're bound to say "Geez, he's weird." Not much of him is known, but think about a teen with an adult mind who's still a little thirteen-year-old kid. Basically, if an adult and a thirteen-year-old did the fusion move from *Dragon Ball Z*, that would be Christian Quevedo. He has a YouTube Channel. You'll learn a lot from him over there.

ROMAN RAMIREZ, age thirteen, grade eight, is currently at Zapata Academy on the South Side of Chicago. Roman is a good boy and tries to stay out of trouble as much as possible. He has been inspired by Brian Urlacher and is now playing football. Roman has been through so much, losing two family members who were too young, but he still has them in his heart and knows they're watching him. He loves eating, math, and Paola.

JESUS AYALA + CHRISTIAN BENITEZ & MARCO HERNANDEZ

Dear Jesus,

Hello, this is my first letter to you. We have some stuff in common and hopefully can know each other more. Here are some questions for you:

- Do you have a series of books or music that you like?
- List three to five songs you like so I can hear them.
- Do you like video games?
- What kind of chips do you like?
- How is your school over there?
- What languages can you speak?
- Do you watch YouTube, and if so, can you list some YouTubers that you watch? I watch YouTube and I want to be a YouTuber.
- I like Mexican songs and *corridos*. Do you like that kind of music? If not, you should hear it. The beats of the songs are on point.

Sincerely,
Marco Hernandez

P.S. Sorry for the little writing, I didn't have much time and didn't know what to write in my sloppy handwriting.

Dear Marco,

From Jesus: What up, Marco? I like corndogs. Nosotros somos buenos pasos. The kind of music I like is rap. For example, Logic and Immortal Technique. I like these two because the lyrics are deep and I like the way they rap. I recommend you listen to "Dance with the Devil," "Dear God," and "Gang Related." I also watch YouTube videos. I like to watch Dashie Games, Pretty Boy Fredo, and Fail Army.

From Christian: I speak Spanish. The games I like to play are *Call of Duty: Black Ops 2*, and *FIFA 15*. My favorite chips are Takis.

From Jesus: I made some questions for you. Do you play any sports? If so, please identify them. What are your favorite subjects? My favorite subject is band. Do you like cars?

From Christian: Do you play any games? What's your favorite song? Do you like any books?

Dear Jesus and Christian,

I was so excited to receive your letter. You seem funny by the way you said things. Can you name some singers or songs you like? I will listen to them and give you feedback about the songs. I have some questions for you: are you guys friends with each other, and if so, how did you meet?

Do you ever miss being a small kid and not worrying about a lot of things? Just watching TV and your parents not saying "Do your homework! Clean up?" Well, I do. The best thing I could do was to watch *Bob the Builder* all day. I would also play and just wait for my dad to get home. The best day was my birthday when my dad got home and surprised me with more toys to play with. What was the best time of your life?

How are you doing? I haven't heard much about you. How is high school? How has it changed for you? Can you describe your school? I can't wait to go to high school.

Sincerely,
Marco

Dear Marco,

I sometimes do miss being a small kid. I miss not worrying about doing homework or having to help clean around the house. The best thing to do as a kid was play with my toy cars, which I still have.

The best time of my life was when I went to Six Flags for the first time. Have you ever been to Six Flags? This was the best time of my life because it was my first time being in an amusement park. I went with my mom, aunt, cousins, and my uncle. I was about twelve years old at the time. The first ride I ever went on was the American Eagle. I was scared at first, but it wasn't as bad as I thought it would be. I liked when the roller coaster was going up because you could see almost all the park from that height. That day it was about ninety degrees so we wanted to end the day with the water rides.

Sincerely,
Christian B.

"Now let me tell you, the best time of my life was when I got onto my first roller coaster."

Dear Marco,

I agree with you about missing being a kid. I would just go play soccer and basketball outside, but now we're growing up and we are going to have to be mature. I am trying to find a job so I can get money to help my parents pay some bills. I want to buy stuff for my sister, brother, and parents. I'm looking for a job, like as a busboy where my dad works. It's called L. Woods. When I get my own money I want to buy my own clothes and shoes. I'm looking into buying my own car.

Now let me tell you, the best time of my life was when I got onto my first roller coaster. I was like seven or eight years old, and I was so ready for this. I was looking forward for it all summer. When I was next in line for the Raging Bull, I started having second thoughts, but then I said YOLO, I'm going on that ride! I started getting nervous every time we went higher. I held on tight on my seat. Then the drop came and I started to scream. I actually could hardly even scream because the air was going inside my mouth so fast. After that ride I was too scared to get on any other ride the whole day. Now I still get on rides but not that often really.

All right, Marco, that was the end of my story. Hope I get to see you soon.

Sincerely,
Jesus

JESUS AYALA is a bilingual Mexican student at Amundsen High School. He is sixteen years old and likes to play baseball, basketball, and soccer.

CHRISTIAN BENITEZ is a sophomore in Chicago who likes to play soccer and volleyball for fun. His favorite movies are *Hacksaw Ridge*, *Fury*, and *Now You See Me 2*. He knows how to play the french horn. He wants to join the military in the future.

MARCO HERNANDEZ lives in Chicago's Little Village. He is thirteen years old and is in eighth grade. He hates coffee. The only drink he likes from McDonald's is their strawberry banana smoothie. His favorite YouTuber is DavidParody, a funny guy. Marco is very good at *Call of Duty: Black Ops 3* but hates writing.

SONGS THAT HAVE BEEN THERE FOR ME

From our authors:

- "BOUNCE BACK" — BIG SEAN
- "BEETLE JUICE" — CHIEF KEEF
- "NO ROLE MODELZ" — J COLE
- "FAITHFUL" — DRAKE
- "CALM DOWN" — YOUNG PUPPY
- "SOUL FOOD" — LOGIC
- "NO I DO WHAT I WANT" — LIL UZI VERT
- "PIANO CONCIERTO NO. 1" — TCHAIKOVSKY

Here are mine:

_____

_____

_____

_____

_____

YES, I'VE DANCED IN THE MIRROR TO ALL OF THESE

From our authors:

- "NEW YEARS DAY" — PENTATONIX
- "BY THE WAY" — RED HOT CHILI PEPPERS
- "STORY" — KANA NISHINO
- "EARNED IT" — THE WEEKND
- "FAMILY BUSINESS" — KANYE WEST
- "CUTE WITHOUT THE 'E' (CUT FROM THE TEAM)" — TAKING BACK SUNDAY
- "THUNDERSTRUCK" — AC/DC
- "GIVES YOU HELL" — ALL-AMERICAN REJECTS

Here are mine:

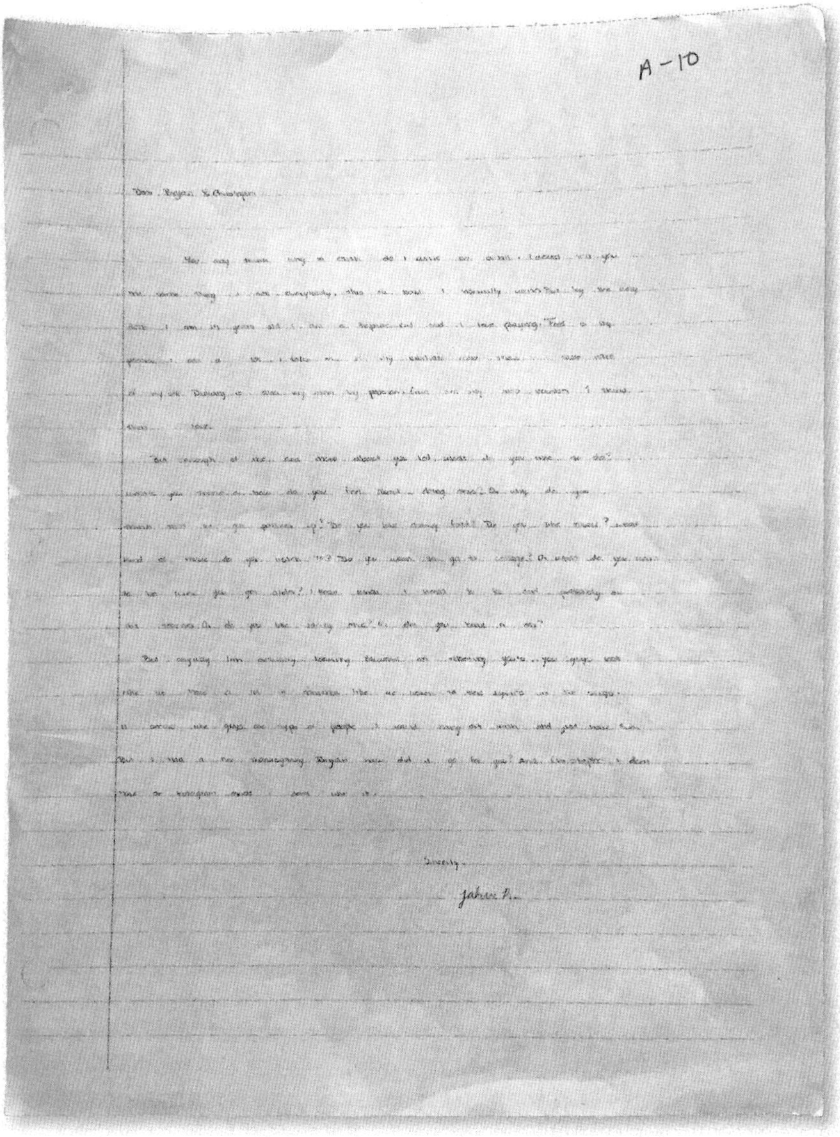

A-10

Dear Bryan & Christopher

[illegible]

Sincerely,

CHRISTOPHER RIVERA + BRYAN VILLEGAS & JAHIR REBOLLEDO

Dear Bryan and Christopher,

You may wonder why on earth I write so small. I would tell you the same thing I tell everybody: this is how I normally write. By the way: I am fourteen years old, I am a Hispanic kid, and I love playing. Food is my passion. I eat a lot. I take care of my siblings more than I take care of myself. Drawing is my other big passion. Cars are the number one thing that I love.

But enough of me and more about you, LOL. What do you like to do? How do you feel about doing this? Or, why do you think that we got partnered up? Do you love eating food? What kind of music do you listen to? Do you want to go to college? What do you want to be when you get older? I know what I want to be, probably an art teacher. Do you like racing cars? Do you have a car?

I'm actually looking forward to meeting you. It looks like we have a lot in common, like we listen especially to the lyrics in songs. It seems like you guys are the type of people I would hang out and just have fun with.

Sincerely,
Jahir R.

"I want to be an astronomer or astronaut because I want to discover and explore the final frontier ♥."

Dear Jahir,

You sound like an interesting person. Christopher and I are in the tenth grade, we're both in robotics club, and we like cars too. Christopher likes rap music and I like classical. What kind of music do you like? Christopher wants to be an aerospace engineer, and I want to be an astronomer or astronaut. Christopher and I are from Hispanic/Latino descent too. Christopher's favorite food is empanadas, and my favorite food is sushi or any other Asian food. Christopher wants to be an aerospace engineer because he does rocketry competitions with the STEM Club at Amundsen and plans to work with bigger rockets. I would want to be an astronomer or astronaut because I want to discover and explore the final frontier ♥.

Sincerely,
Christopher and Bryan

Dear Bryan and Christopher,

Well, hi once again! How's STEM Club, Christopher? How are your competitions going? I forgot to ask you guys something last time: do you like dancing? Bryan, why are you interested in being an astronomer or astronaut? Do you guys play sports? I know I do. I play soccer and volleyball, but I play soccer a lot more. I have been playing since I was five years old.

Does either of you guys have a car? Or what kind of cars are you guys into? The best day of my life was when I started driving because I learned on a stick shift car. It was a Porsche. I'm usually more into foreign cars like the Scion FRS. They're small cars, but I'm looking forward to getting into races. Do you guys work? Over my summer I did and that's why I love cars.

I like some kinds of rap, but I'm more into bands. I don't know what else to say, but right now my mind is blank. I literally don't know anything this early in the morning.

A special place to me is my room because people think it's messy, but it's actually very organized to me. When you take a smell, you get a sense of vanilla. It's very cold. It's also very loud because I always have music on. Do you guys have a special place? What are you thinking about right now at this moment?

Sincerely,
Jahir R.

Dear Jahir,

It's nice hearing from you again. I'm just going to start off by answering some of your questions. Robotics Club is actually going great. We haven't done a lot of competitions, but in the ones that we have had, we placed very well. When it comes to sports, I have played a lot, but my favorite is wrestling.

Now that both of our questions are answered by each other, it would be cool to know something about you, like a story. I'll start. I started wrestling when I was in sixth grade and I loved it, so I joined my school team the next year. I did pretty well, but during the state tournament I tore my ACL. It was literally like twenty minutes after I won that a kid—I'm not sure if it was on purpose—kicked my knee in. They took me to the hospital and there I was told that I had torn my ACL. It took a while to get back to my normal self after the surgeries, but it was okay because I still got to wrestle the next year. I had to wear some weird brace. It was pretty much a scary experience, but it really humbled me because it helped me figure out that everyone's good time doesn't last.

Now, I want to hear from you. I'm excited to see what you have to say.

Sincerely,
Chris

Dear Jahir,

I have gotten your letter and thought it was interesting. Now, I'm going to tell a story that is tragic.

It was March 2, 2010. It was a chilly and sunny day in Chicago. I had just come back from school. My sister was taking care of me and my little brother. I was very tired that day, so I sat down with him to play *Call of Duty: Black Ops 1* on the PS3.

When it was dinner time, my sister called my brother and me to eat. After we were done eating, my older brother, Wally, always played cello with flair. The pieces my brother played were extremely rigorous, because it was really hard to get around the notes and dynamics to make it sound beautiful.

Me and my little brother were playing with toy soldiers when we started to notice a burning smell coming from the living room. We immediately told our older brother and sister. The source of the smell was coming from our heater. We quickly got water and poured it all over, but that did not work. Seconds later, the black, ominous smoke grew bigger and more intimidating, so we left our home and went to the backyard. It was a horrible feeling watching our home engulfed in flames.

When my godparents found out about the fire, they housed us for roughly a month while we were looked for a new home.

Sincerely,
Bryan

Dear Bryan and Chris,

Hello! I've actually had the same experience as both of you!

Chris, getting surgery is not the best. I mean, for me having surgery was horrible because I wasn't able to play soccer for almost five months. Also, I had these special nails in my body that held my thumb in place. It was very painful because it was during the winter, and the nails would get so cold that they would freeze my thumb.

Bryan, I've also lived your experience. My house burned too, but it wasn't as bad as yours because I wasn't home when my house burned. I was at my soccer game, but I found out about it an hour later. It was horrible, and the worst part was that, once I got home, I wasn't able to save any of my belongings. We all lost everything we had. I'm doing better now though, and it doesn't get to me as much as it used to.

I think it was pretty brave for both of you to share your memories with me. Thank you for sharing.

Sincerely,
Jahir R.

Dear Jahir,

I love when I get your letters. It really does make my day because you help me understand that there is someone out there who actually understands what I went through. It sucks that this might be the last letter we send each other. I am really going to miss your stories, but I guess I can leave you with one more.

Last year, which was my freshman year, I tried to wrestle again. I didn't really do that well. I lost every single match. I pretty much lost all hope for myself when it came to wrestling, but I didn't completely give up because of my coach. He told me to stay and gave me advice on how to fix what I was doing wrong.

For that whole week I practiced harder than ever and finally won my first match. I had nineteen losses and one win. That win encouraged me to try harder, and my sophomore year I ended up winning seventeen times and only had four losses. The reason I told you this story is because you are going to high school. I don't want you to give up on whatever you do. Just do what what you like and keep going.

Sincerely,
Chris

P.S. BTW that is a nice elephant.

CHRISTOPHER RIVERA is sixteen years old and goes to Amundsen High School. A few interesting things about him are that he wrestles, he likes to travel, and he likes to eat different foods. When he grows up, he wants to be an aerospace engineer.

BRYAN VILLEGAS is a sophomore at Amundsen High School. He has a passion for cello. His favorite type of music is classical music: Shostakovich, Vivaldi, Beethoven, Tchaikovsky, Bach, Chopin. He hates any sweet food or drinks. Bryan's future career will be either a music teacher, astronomer, or astronaut. Bryan's favorite hero is Iron Man. He has been a fan of Iron Man since he was six. If Bryan could have any power it would be super intelligence because with that power he could solve most of the world's problems.

JAHIR REBOLLEDO is fifteen years old. He lives in and comes from Little Village. He loves anything on pizza except pineapple. He is not a morning person. He's small but big in what he loves to do. He's rude but can be so gentle when he has to. He was once boring, shy, and a very independent person. He would love to go on to play soccer and give his family a better life.

SHIVAM PATEL & JOSHUA FLORES

Dear Shivam Patel,

My name is Joshua. I like Mexican food. I am in a rock band. I have played soccer since I was six years old. I have a little sister who gets me in trouble all the time, but she is smart. My dad is also a really hard worker and he said that I have to be good at something to get a job.

I have some questions. Do you like school? Why or why not? Do you speak Spanish? What's your favorite food or restaurant?

Sincerely,
Joshua Flores

Dear Joshua,

It's nice to be able to write to you again so I can learn about you. When I first came to high school I didn't really think I would play an instrument, like an alto saxophone, until I actually began to play and enjoy it. I have an older sister who has been playing the violin here in high school and is going to graduate this year. I also really enjoy playing video games like *Call of Duty*, *Grand Theft Auto V*, and *FIFA*. I also like playing soccer like you do.

To answer your questions, I really like my school because I get to meet new people and learn interesting things. High school is really interesting because unlike in middle school, every class has a lot of different students who you can become friends with. Finally, my favorite type of food is Mexican food, even though I am from India.

I would also like to ask you questions. What role do you play in your band? What position do you play in soccer? What do you imagine high school is like? Do you have any more questions for me? For now, while I await your questions, I will talk about the biggest thing to happen in my life.

I was around three years old when it happened, but I can remember that it was at night, before my sister and I fell asleep. We were playing *Duck Hunt* against each other when we heard noise from outside the bedroom. I opened the door and saw paramedics rushing into my parents' bedroom. My grandparents and my mother were watching whatever the paramedics were doing with tears in their eyes. My sister and I went into my parents' room and I saw the paramedics all around my dad where he was lying on the bed, but we were rushed back out. My sister and I were scared after seeing it, so we just began to cry silently. A couple days later, I found out my dad had died of cancer.

It wasn't until I was around eight and in the third grade that I fully got over this because I began to do art. I also made friends (that I still have today) who helped to get me as far as I have come. Though I don't draw often anymore, I am now in Advanced Band, which has been of great help to me. I was also wondering, Joshua, what is the thing that helps you get through life?

From,
Shivam Patel

Dear Shivam,

Thank you for the letter. It was really sad. I'm so sorry about your dad's death. What helps me get through life is my rock band and guitar club. Also, what helps me get through life is my dad because he is always there when I need him.

I have experienced a really close death in my family. My grandfather fell down the stairs and was in the hospital for a whole week. It was the last week of school, and I remember that Sunday my dad stayed home from work because it was Father's Day. My mom got a call from Mexico and we learned that my grandfather had died. When I heard, I stayed in my room for two days. I was so sad. I am telling you this because I think I know how you feel. It was really nice to read your letter.

What was the thing that you liked the most about your dad?

Sincerely,
Joshua

Dear Joshua,

I feel bad about your grandfather's death, even though none of my grandparents have passed. However, I can still relate to the emotions you felt because of my father's death. It's a good thing that your rock band helps you get through it.

To answer your question, one of my best memories with my dad was when I went fishing with him because fishing was one of his passions. We would always walk a mile to a pier in the afternoon to go fishing. I remembered catching a fish twice my size and giving pieces of fish to all of my relatives in the apartment building we lived in.

I would like to ask you, Joshua, what do you remember about your grandfather? How much time did you spend with him? How long has it been since he passed away?

Sincerely,
Shivam

SHIVAM PATEL is a fifteen-year-old sophomore and musician. He enjoys playing video games whenever he can and uploads videos to YouTube every week. He used to draw and was really lazy, but he has changed over the years. He would like to be a big YouTuber, professional musician, or professional gamer. His favorite subject is math and he loves to watch anime.

JOSHUA FLORES is fourteen years old. He lives in Chicago and goes to Emiliano Zapata. He is known as Mr. Flowers. He really likes to play guitar and is in a rock band. He has a dog that is labrador-pit bull mix. He is funny and would like to be part of a rock band when he grows up.

SPEND 60 SECONDS LISTING EVERYTHING YOU CAN THINK OF FOR EACH OF THE FOLLOWING:

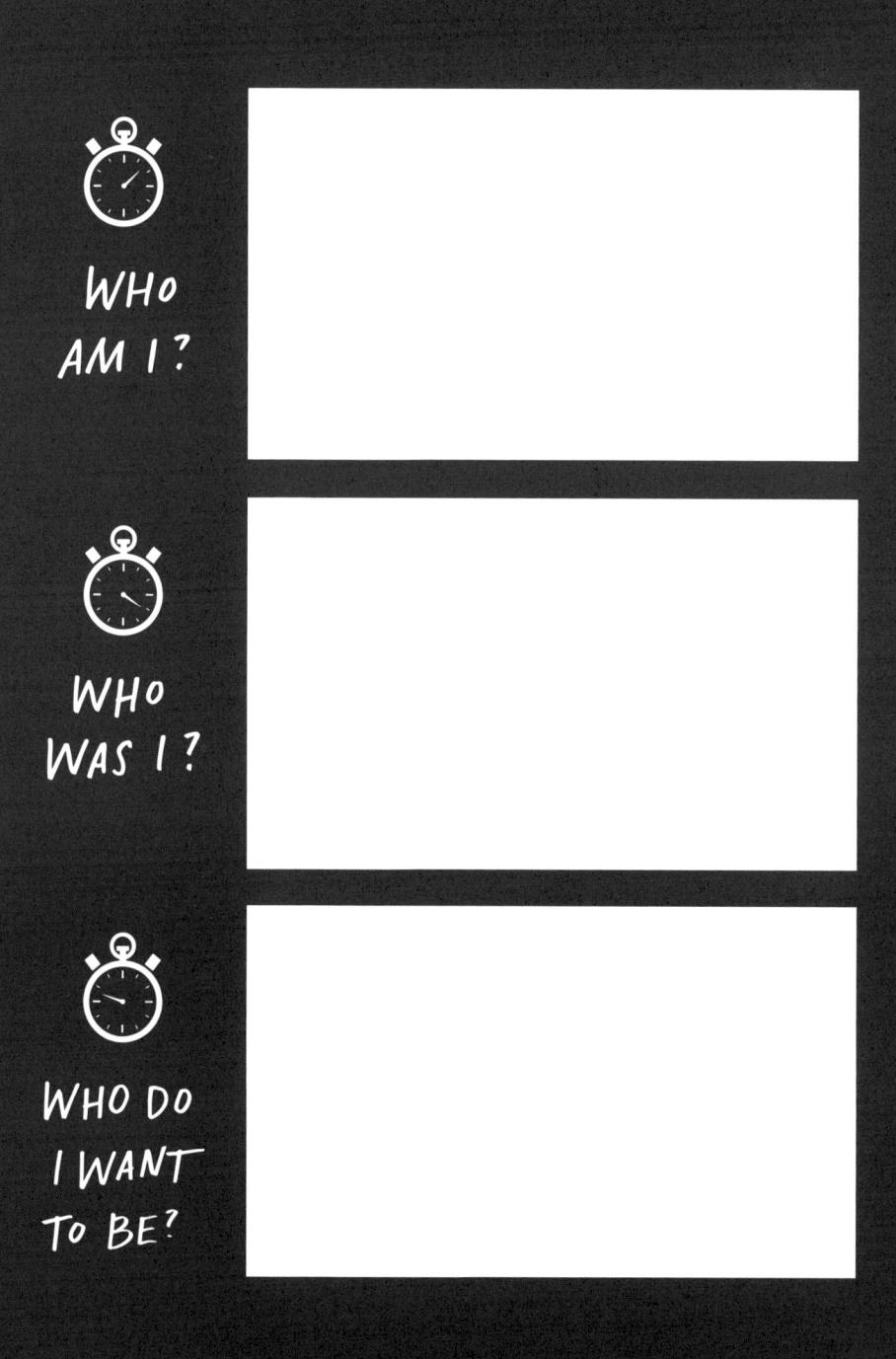

WHO AM I?

WHO WAS I?

WHO DO I WANT TO BE?

SOHAIL NAZARI & INOCENTE DIRCIO

Dear Sohail,

My name is Inocente. How have you been? I saw on the survey that you prefer to read manga. I do too! One of my favorite mangas is *Naruto*, and my favorite anime is *Tokyo Ghost*. I also like to draw a lot. Was Amundsen High School your first choice? Was your freshman year easy for you? What kind of music are you into? I like Twenty One Pilots.

One of the best days of my life so far was on a family trip when I was little. We went into this lake and I almost drowned. To be honest, I don't know why I thought it was funny, but when I came out of the water I was laughing. I think the real best day of my life will be when I'm in high school or college because I will get to meet new people who may be from different places.

Something that's on my mind right now is a quote from a poem. The quote says, "Death inspires me like a dog inspires a rabbit." I have had this quote and the words of the whole poem in my head because I can relate to it. Have you ever thought about or paid attention to a poem or a song closely?

What's something or someone you want or don't want to be in the future? For example, something or someone I don't want to be is Normal because, like this quote I read, *Normal people scare me*. And to be honest, they do. I'm personally very weird and I don't want to be a normal, serious person. I'm sometimes a sad person, but yeah, I don't know. I hope to talk to you soon.

Sincerely,
Inocente D.

Dear Inocente,

My name is Sohail. I am in the tenth grade. *Naruto* is also one of my favorite mangas. I have tons of favorite animes, but I have a few top ones: *Bleach*, *Death Note*, *7 Deadly Sins*, and *One Piece*. I like drawing, but I am personally really bad at it. The high school I am in now was my first choice because my sister came here and told me great things about it. Sadly, she graduated three years ago.

Asked about my favorite family trip, I think I would have to say it was when I went to this place called Starved Rock. It's about two hours away from Chicago and it's really beautiful. What was your favorite family trip? Why was it your favorite?

I want to tell you about this time I met a stranger. One day I met an old man, probably around the age of sixty or seventy. He asked me if I played any sports. I told him I didn't, and that I'm just honestly too lazy to go out and play. He told me something I will not forget, ever.

He told me, "Look, I am a really old man and I'm grown up. I have kids and grandkids. I lived a long and good life, but if I could go back and change one thing in my life, it would be to play more sports. Trust me, once you get to an age where you can't do these things anymore, you'll realize that you should have played more sports while you could. My advice to you is to go out every summer and play a new sport. Have as much fun as you can, so once you grow old, you can tell your grandkids stories of how many sports you played, unlike me." Then he laughed. "Trust me, you'll eventually find a rival who you will compete with and have lots of fun with."

After that day I went out and played a new sport every summer. I also found my rival, LOL. My advice to you, Inocente, is to go out and have fun while you can. I've played many sports and I've loved all of them: soccer, basketball, ping pong, football.

By the way, have you ever gotten into a cool interaction with a stranger? What do you like to do in your free time? I'd like to hear some cool stories from you too! Until next time, peace!

Sincerely,
Sohail

P.S. You should watch this anime called *Code Geass*.

Dear Sohail,

Some things I like to do in my free time are draw, listen to music, think, walk, and ride my bike different places. Something kind of interesting that happened last Saturday is that me and two friends were at the park, and we decided to climb a small building. The thing is, my friend Anthony had never climbed the building before. We literally spent half an hour trying to get him up in different ways until we finally could get him up. In the process of getting him up, my ribs started hurting and my hand got scratched. It started bleeding. When we wanted to get down it was easy, except for Anthony who fell off. Luckily, he was okay.

I don't know if this counts as an interaction with a stranger, but I met someone from the United Kingdom, a girl that goes by Caire. I didn't meet her in real life but in the internet. We video chatted, texted, and called. She taught me a lot of stuff about life and most of the things I like now are because of her. I remember I didn't like anything at all, but she helped me get through problems and she told me, "Don't let someone ruin your day."

Sincerely,
Inocente D.

Dear Inocente,

I had a great time reading your letter! I found it kind of funny that your friend spent so much time trying to climb the building. I'm glad Anthony is okay.

Me and my friends always climb this one building. It's scary because there's this one part where to climb onto the roof you have to use a ladder that's connected to the wall. If you make one small mistake you could fall and possibly even die. But it's worth it because, once you've climbed it, you have this incredible feeling that you've accomplished something. When we climb up there we have a clear view of the Chicago skyline and city lights.

My advice to you is don't ever let someone ruin your day, life, week, anything. Do you and don't worry what anyone thinks. Have a nice school year and summer break!

Sincerely,
Sohail

SOHAIL NAZARI is a fifteen-year-old teenager who goes to Amundsen High School. He is a very quick learner and plays many sports. He gets very competitive when it comes to sports and the things he likes. He is also sarcastic and funny. He has a small circle of friends and those who are in it are considered his family. His goals are to become an electrical engineer, a great son to his parents, and a great brother for his friends and family to count on when they need to.

INOCENTE DIRCIO, grade eight, attends to Zapata Emiliano Academy and lives in a house in Chicago. He likes to watch a lot of anime. One of his favorites is *Tokyo Ghoul*. He likes McDonald's and likes the McChicken a lot. He also likes Celis Pizzeria because sometimes they give him discounts. Inocente is someone who would take a bag of Takis to school and eat them in the bathroom to not get caught. He is also the type of person who eats a lot. He likes a lot of music, enjoys the nighttime, and is mostly in the streets.

CUNG LIEU & KRYSTAL NAMBO

Dear Cung Lieu,

My name is Krystal Nambo and I am thirteen years old. My birthday is June 11. I grew up in a Hispanic and not-so-safe community. I say not-so-safe because there are a lot of gun shots at night, so it is better if you don't walk home alone.

I currently attend Zapata Academy and hope to graduate to move up to high school. I enjoy being active and playing sports, even though I may not be good at them. My passion is dance and I have been taking dance classes since I was four years old. I am a happy person who likes to try new things and have adventures. I also like nature, art, listening to music, and watching my favorite TV show.

I would like to ask a few questions. When is your birthday? Do you play any sports? What is your favorite TV show? What was your freshman year like? Favorite memory? I saw that you think lyrics are the most important thing in a song. I agree with you.

Have a good day! I can't wait to meet you face-to-face.

Sincerely,
Krystal

Dear Krystal Nambo,

I am Cung Lieu and I am happy to have gotten your letter. I am seventeen years old and my birthday is on September 25. My community is a safe and peaceful place. I attend Amundsen High School. I play a lot of sports, but football is my favorite sport to play. My favorite memory was this year when I was on the football team and we won six straight games to end the season. The positions I play are middle linebacker and outside linebacker.

I want to tell you something a little personal that happened to me in eighth grade. In eighth grade, I was happy and excited because when school started I got to see my friends again. (As you know, I don't go out much.) I also got to see the girl I liked. Her name was Maria. I was disappointed because she was in a different classroom than I was. I'd liked her for a long time, but I was scared to know how she felt about me, so I didn't say anything for a long time. We were friends and we talked all year. Then last year, I found out she had a boyfriend. When I found out about that, it felt like my chest was going to burst. The worst part was that I found out about it from him, not her. That was last year, so I got over it. I was happy just seeing her happy, but I was still too cowardly to tell her how I felt.

Then, one day, I was at home. We were texting each other, talking about normal stuff. She mentioned that her boyfriend had told her that I liked her. I was so angry at him, but when I saw her reply I felt devastated. Her response was: "I only like you as a good friend." My heart felt like it fell out of my body, sitting there lifeless. I didn't reply to her for a while. She asked if I was okay. I replied, "I'm fine and see you at school tomorrow." The next day I woke up still with the same terrible feeling. I washed up, got dressed, and went to school.

When I saw her waiting around for me, I didn't look her in the eye or anything. For the whole day I didn't say a word to her. She texted me later to ask how I was, and even though I wasn't fine, I sucked it up and told her I was okay. This continued until we graduated from eighth grade, and now we haven't talked to each other in over a year. I learned that day that there are things in life that, no matter how hard you try, you can never get.

Sincerely,
Cung Lieu

Dear Cung Lieu,

I'm sorry this happened to you. Your story was interesting, but at the end you said, "There are things in life that, no matter how hard you try, you can never get," and I don't think that is true. I think it just takes time, or you have to wait for the right moment, or sometimes you have to try harder.

What is one crazy memory you have? I remember once I went to the store with my mom, my brother, and my aunts because we were going to buy party decorations for my grandma's surprise party. Me and my brother were running around and playing even though our mom told us not to, practicing karate tricks and running around like crazy. My brother threw a bouncy ball at me, but he missed and knocked down cups of glass that ended up shattering everywhere! We left the store as soon as I told my mom what happened. She was so mad—I was so scared I'd get in trouble. After that I learned to obey my parents and to be careful when I'm at the store. Do you have any similar memories?

I have a few last questions for you. What's your favorite movie? Do you have a favorite YouTuber? What were some of your struggles in your freshman year of high school? Since this is our last letter, I want to say goodbye and it was nice writing to you.

Sincerely,
Krystal Nambo

Dear Krystal Nambo,

Now that I heard what you thought about the ending of my story, I am starting to change my mind and agree with you. Thank you for your thoughts.

I have one memory as a little kid that was really weird. I don't remember how old I was, but I was at my uncle's house having a small barbecue party with friends and family. We were having fun and eating. It was pretty loud, but not as loud as an all-out party. The day went by and it was time for me, my brother, and sister to go home. One of my uncle's friends who is my friend too asked us to give him a kiss to the cheek. My brother and sister were fine when they did it, but when I tried to do it, he turned his head and I kissed him on the lips instead of the cheek. That's when I learned not to trust everyone. It was embarrassing and everyone laughed. After that we left and went back home. I still see him from time to time.

I really don't have a favorite movie. My favorite YouTuber is VanossGaming. His videos are all funny because he edits the videos he records and with his friends the videos become funnier. It takes a while for him to post videos, but when he does, most of the time it's worth waiting for.

In my freshman year, there wasn't really anything that I struggled with. I think that homework was a little bit of a struggle. Overall, it was okay for me in freshman year. Well, thank you for your time. I'm happy to have been writing to you. Have a good day and goodbye.

Sincerely,
Cung Lieu

P.S. Nice decorations on your paper.

CUNG LIEU is seventeen years old. He loves to play football and any other sports. He hates basketball and homework. He's quiet most of the time. He also plays video games in his free time or just watches movies.

KRYSTAL NAMBO, age thirteen, is a strange girl because she talks to herself sometimes when she is bored. Krystal enjoys eating a lot when it's something she likes, and sometimes even mixes different foods to see how it tastes. Krystal's safe place is in her room with paper, where she can express her thoughts and feelings. She doesn't say much but watches and keeps her thoughts to herself. Fun fact: she never talked in first or second grade. Writing has always been a favorite for Krystal because she can be herself and write the truth. Sometimes she wishes that she could visit and travel all over the world to discover new places and make memories. She has always been curious and wonders what the future has in store for her. She used to be a scared girl, but now she is somewhat brave.

DULCE RIVERA + IVAN ALVAREZ & EDUARDO GAMBOA

Dear Dulce,

My name is Eduardo Gamboa. I am an eighth grader attending Zapata Academy. I am taking high school algebra. My favorite hobbies are using my phone to play games and playing video games on my Xbox One. I don't use social media because I think people waste too much time on it. My favorite activities in school are math and gym. My favorite sports are volleyball and cross country.

I have some questions that I would like you to answer. How old are you? What is your favorite sport? Any hobbies? What is your favorite thing to do in school? What is your favorite food?

When you write back to me, I hope I can relate to you. I am worried about change when I enter high school, but I feel I can overcome it. Like you, I like to plan my day out in the morning because I want to be prepared for the future.

I really can't wait to see you face-to-face to talk about some more things. See you later.

Sincerely,
Eduardo Gamboa

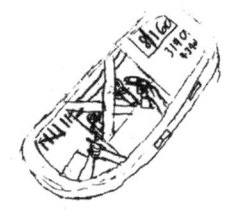

Dear Eduardo,

My name is Dulce Rivera and I go to Amundsen High School. I'm fifteen years old, but I'm about to turn sixteen in a few weeks. One of my favorite sports would have to be ice skating, even though I don't do it that often anymore. Another sport would be skateboarding, if that counts.

Some of my favorite hobbies are listening to music or playing some of my favorite instruments, like violin or piano. My favorite thing about school is playing in orchestra and in after school clubs like Anime Club or Video Game Club. Speaking of video games, what have you played? Some of my favorite games are *Battlefront* and *Fallout 4* on PS4. My current favorite food is pizza because it's the only thing I can think of.

Anyway, what music do you like? What bands? I like bands like Fall Out Boy, The Story So Far, Pierce the Veil, and Sleeping with Sirens. My current favorite band is a band called Waterparks. I recommend them.

Sincerely,
Dulce Rivera

Dear Eduardo Gamboa,

Hello, I'm Ivan. I'm sixteen years old. My favorite sport is soccer. One hobby I have is playing *Call of Duty* on the PS4. My favorite thing to do in school is have some fun with my friends. My favorite food is tacos. The position I play in soccer is left wing or left back. I'm not so good at turning in my homework on time. One show that I started to like is *Arrow*. What would your future job be? Nice writing to you.

Sincerely,
Ivan Alvarez

Dear Ivan and Dulce,

I will answer all of your questions first. I want two jobs in the future: I want to be an engineer and a chef. I want to be a chef because I cook with my mom, and I want to be an engineer because I build things with Legos.

I have two favorite bands: Dutty Moonshine and Queens of the Stone Age. My favorite game is *Call of Duty: Black Ops 3*, but I play Zombies most of the time. I don't prefer PS4 because I was used to Xbox 360 controls when it came out. I have an Xbox One.

The high school I plan on attending is either Whitney Young or Little Village Infinity. I want to go to Infinity more because my sister says a lot of nice things about her school. She says her teachers are very supportive.

I have a few questions for both of you. Dulce, what are your favorite feelings when you play an instrument? Ivan, what clubs are you in? For both of you: what college do you plan on going to or not? Why or why not do you want to attend college?

I have two stories to tell. First, if I could switch lives with my parents I would, because I've always wanted to get paid for working. But I don't want to take care of my little brothers.

The second story is about how my phone was stolen at Home Depot. I was with my father. We were walking down an aisle when a man tripped me and I fell. The guy helped me up and walked away. Ten minutes later, I realized my phone was missing. I found the guy outside trying to unlock my phone, so I called security to help me. They kicked him out and I got my phone back. Hope you enjoyed my letters and had a great Christmas break.

Happy New Year,
Eduardo Gamboa

Dear Eduardo,

How is it going? In your last letter you asked how I felt while playing music. I honestly feel a lot of emotions. Some days I feel happiness, sadness, anger, and so many other feelings. It just really depends on the moment.

I've got a question for you: what are some of your favorite conspiracy theories or urban legends? Mine are the mothman, aliens, and that the landing on the moon was fake. I mean, they seem crazy at first, but when it's 4 a.m. and you haven't slept in a long time, they make a lot more sense.

One time, when I was a kid, I went on a field trip to a U.S. Air Force base. It was a five day trip that only happened during school hours. The base was in South Carolina. I can't really remember the name of it, but I grew up close to the base and I remember hearing the planes fly by. I remember that I used to mistake some of the airplanes for UFOs. Anyway, on the trip we spent five days learning about science, and they had us build little, tiny rockets. The last day of the trip was probably the most fun because we got to launch them.

We also got really cool dog tags. We got to see some of the aircrafts and equipment they had. It was really cool and awesome. I remember being able to put on night vision goggles. They only had a few so the class had to take turns. When it was my turn, I used it to scare fellow classmates who couldn't see in the dark. That field trip really inspired me, and thanks to it I really want to become a pilot.

Talk to you soon,
Dulce Rivera

Dear Dulce,

I am writing to you to tell you some great things. I am going on my eighth grade trip to a camp site, and it will be a three-day stay. I can't wait to go. This will sadly be my last letter to you.

So, there's this girl in my class who I danced with on Valentine's at our school dance. Who did I dance with? I won't say her name, but she is really pretty. My question to you is what do you think I should get her for a gift? I really want to impress her and I want to get her something nice.

Take care and see you in a couple of weeks!

Eduardo Gamboa

Dear Eduardo,

I think you should do some investigating and find out what she likes. I used to be an Xbox fan, but my brother bought me a PS4 instead. Learning to play PS4 was a big change for me because I wasn't used to the controllers. I like to play soccer in the summer outside. I love the challenge of trying to be the best player. I also like to go outside when it's not so cold and hot. I also like to nap for three hours daily.

Sincerely,
Ivan Alvarez

Dear Eduardo,

Hey, it's really sad that this is my last letter to you. Your eighth grade trip seems so cool. Mine was just a trip downtown, which was lame but kind of cool at the same time. Anyway, the girl that you danced with must be pretty cool, I recommend getting her something you know she is going to like, or you could just get her flowers or something like that.

Recently I've been really excited about some upcoming events I have. I managed to buy my badges for ACen and Anime Midwest, which are pretty cool anime conventions. The only thing I'm worried about is if I'm going to finish my cosplays on time. I'm going to be cosplaying Noctis from *Final Fantasy 15*, plus Lance and Keith from *Voltron: Legendary Defenders*. I've also got a Bring Me the Horizon concert soon. I also get to meet one of my favorite YouTubers, MilesChronicles. So, this is a pretty exciting time for me right now.

I really can't wait to meet you. I bet it's going to be really fun. Good luck with the girl. I hope the advice I gave you helped.

See you soon,
Dulce Rivera

DULCE RIVERA is a sixteen-year-old kid who likes *Final Fantasy 15* and *Voltron* more than herself. Her favorite bands are Waterparks and BTS. In her free time she cosplays or hangs out with friends. When she grows up, she wants to be a comic book artist.

IVAN ALVAREZ is sixteen years old and lives in Chicago. Ivan loves to play soccer and PS4. He wishes Malcolm in the Middle had never ended. He wishes everybody could enjoy tacos the way he does. He loves to spend time with his friends and go to random places. He really doesn't enjoy any subject in school. He has one brother and one sister. Both are older than him.

EDUARDO GAMBOA is a thirteen-year-old eighth grader at Zapata Academy and has been in Chicago his whole life. Eduardo likes graphic novels about Deadpool and The Simpsons. He also likes video games about first-person shooters, like *Call of Duty: Black Ops 3*. He is a zombie-killing machine. Eduardo prefers to play on Xbox than on PlayStation. He also plans to attend Infinity Math, Science, and Technical High School and will join the cross country team. In the future, he plans to be a video game designer and a chef.

WHAT IS THE FIRST THING YOU THINK ABOUT IN THE MORNING?

WHAT IS THE LAST THING YOU THINK ABOUT AT NIGHT?

DALILA SANCHEZ & JAZMIN ZAMUDIO

Dear Dalila Sanchez,

Hi, my name is Jazmin. I am an eighth grader at Emiliano Zapata Academy. I am a very goofy girl once you get to know me. I love Mexican food and very spicy food.

I love The Weeknd. He is my favorite. I think his voice is amazing and I agree with what you said about him having a pure voice. I'd like to know your top three favorite songs by The Weeknd, besides "Wicked Games."

How is high school? How was your freshman year? Did you have any friends? Are you nervous about taking the SAT next year? How old are you? When is your birthday? Do you play any sports?

My biggest concern right now would be if I graduate or not. What's yours? What kind of classes for college are you going to take? What are you going to study? I want to be a lawyer in the future.

I am looking forward to meeting you.

Sincerely,
Jazmin Zamudio

Dear Jazmin,

Chicago is my city. I'm from the Edgewater neighborhood. Some people like to take walks or swim, but I like to explore abandoned buildings with my two close friends. At the edge of downtown, there's an abandoned factory where it's easy to go inside. As my friends and I sneak in, the ice cold weather goes up a few degrees. The building was constructed mostly from cement and designed in a pattern that seems like a maze. Technically it's illegal to trespass, but what's life without a little risk?

My top three songs by The Weeknd would be "Often," "Starboy," and "Earned It." High school's great if you're consistent with your work. My freshman year made me realize that it didn't matter who I was friends with before. If you're part of a group, slowly it'll fall off little by little. I made friends mostly through my assigned classes.

I'm seventeen and my birthday is September 19, 1999. My concern is who I'm going to fight this year :). Just kidding, I'm concerned about math class.

Sincerely,
Dalila Sanchez
XOXO

"Technically it's illegal to trespass, but what's life without a little risk?"

Dear Dalila Sanchez,

How you been? Have you done anything interesting? My uncle just got married and it sucks because I don't even like the girl, LOL. But it's cool, I guess. As long as he's happy, I'm happy!

What do you plan on doing this summer? Anything fun you would like to do? I want to go to Florida for vacation. I will also be having lots of parties! But, more importantly, I will be focused on graduating and on my fifteenth birthday party!

Do you like any Drake music? If so, what are your top three songs? Did you do anything special on Valentine's Day? *wink wink* I know I did! I had a nice, romantic date with my bed and some food by myself, watching Netflix. Totally great! (Not really.)

I also wanted to know if you would recommend any movies on Netflix? I have nothing to watch! If you like watching funny things, I recommend you watch *Baby Daddy* or *Young and Hungry* on Netflix!

I heard that this is the last letter I'm sending you. I can't wait to meet you and I hope to get a letter back ♥.

Jazmin

Dear Jazmin,

Overall I've been great lately, enjoying my teen years. Congrats on your uncle's marriage! It always takes time to warm up to someone new. You're right, as long as your uncle's happy, that's all that matters. As for summer plans, I want to visit my family in Mexico and spend time with my friends. Maybe a part-time job? ♥ I love Drake's music! Top three favorite songs are "Marvin's Room," "Work (feat. Rihanna)," and "Hotline Bling." On the day of Valentine's I did the exact same thing as you. =)

On Netflix, you should watch *White Girl*, *Final Girl*, and *Hard Candy*. All three start out kind of boring, but they're all good movies. Since this is the last letter you'll get from me: stay humble and always have positive vibes!

Dalila Sanchez
XOXO =) ♥

DALILA SANCHEZ is not sure about what the future holds. Whatever it has to offer, she'll be waiting, and she'll be ready. She's known for her strong attitude.

JAZMIN ZAMUDIO is from Chicago and is a caring person to those who deserve it. She's very girly with a bad attitude. She loves to have fun and to sleep and eat 24/7, but she always likes things to go her way. She wants to be a lawyer who has a big house with kids and an amazing husband. She's the oldest child and will do anything to make her dreams come true.

"I'm realizing now how hard it is to write this letter without any emojis."

SAMANTHA GUTIERREZ & ALEJANDRA ALMARAZ

Dear Samantha,

My name is Alejandra Almaraz. I am fourteen years old. I was born in Chicago and raised all my life in the Little Village neighborhood. Have you been to Little Village?

I am bilingual—Spanish and English. My first language is Spanish. At home, I talk in Spanish to my parents, but my siblings and I always talk in both. In school, I talk to my friends in both, too, yet I talk full English to my teachers. When I was about six years old I didn't know any English at all, so me and my cousin (who only knew Spanish too) started to invent weird words and pretend they were English. Now, looking back and remembering, it makes me laugh. But to be honest, everything makes me laugh. I'm laughing 24/7. I'm realizing now how hard it is to write this letter without any emojis. I haven't written a letter to anyone in like a year and a half. How about you? A fact about me is that I love food ♥. I like trying new food, but seafood is my least favorite.

Questions for you: What college are you planning to attend? What career would you want to pursue? How old is your dog and what is your dog's name? You don't have to answer these questions if you feel like they are too personal, but how long have you been with your boyfriend and how did you guys meet? What is your favorite color? What is your favorite food to eat? What is your favorite beverage? Do you have a favorite restaurant? What is your favorite fruit? What is your favorite candy? Who is your favorite singer? What genres do you listen to? Do you have any siblings? If so, how many? Was Amundsen your top choice for high school? What are the pros and cons of your school?

Hopefully, with your answers to my questions, I will know you better. I'm excited to see and answer the questions you have for me.

Sincerely,
Alejandra Almaraz

December 6, 2016

Dear Alejandra,

Hi my name is Samantha G I am 16 years old. I was born in Chicago, IL. When I was little my parents moved to Arizona, I lived there for 6 years. I moved back to chicago in 4th grade. I am bilingual as well my 1st language is Spanglish. I speak both Spanish & English; However I don't speak Spanish as much as I do English and I understand more than I can say. I live with my mom & my little brother (he is 14 years old & a freshman) also a dog her name is LuLu & she is a pitbull mix. I can't remember when I last wrote a letter but it was recently. In my English class we write plenty. I also love food and I can sort of tolerate seafood but it isn't my favorite either. My dog is 4 years old had her since she was 1. My boyfriend & I have been together for almost... well actually about to be 9 months. We meet freshmen year. I am latina (Guatemalan & Costa Rican) I would describe myself as Fun, Friendly, silly, hard-working and understanding. My favorite color is burgundy & Any form of blue. My favorite food is pizza/chicken nuggets My favorite drink is Ice tea and Chi tea latte. My favorite restuarant is I have no idea My favorite fruit is strawberries. I listen to all genres except country I perfer Alternative. I have 1 brother & 2 half siblings I don't see. My Highschool application process was complicated but Amundsen was sort of my choice. Have any Questions for me about Highschool? Are you scared? nervous? favorite color, food, fruit, animal? Ever been to a concert?

Sincerly,
Samantha G

Dear Alejandra,

Hi, my name is Samantha G. I am sixteen years old. I was born in Chicago, IL. When I was little my parents moved to Arizona. I lived there for six years, then I moved back to Chicago in fourth grade.

I am bilingual too. My first language is Spanish, however I don't speak Spanish as much as I speak English. I can understand more Spanish than I can speak. I live with my mom and my little brother. He is fourteen years old and a freshman. Also, we have a dog. Her name is Lulu and she is a four-year-old pit bull mix.

I can't remember when I last wrote a letter, but it was recently because in my English class we write plenty. I also love food! I can sort of tolerate seafood, but it isn't my favorite either. My boyfriend and I have been together for almost nine months. We met freshman year.

I am a Latina—Guatemalan and Costa Rican. I would describe myself as fun, friendly, silly, hard-working, and understanding. My favorite color is burgundy and any form of blue. My favorite food is pizza or chicken nuggets. My favorite drink is an iced tea or a Chai tea latte. My favorite fruit is strawberries. I listen to all genres of music except country, but I prefer alternative. I have one brother and two half-siblings.

My high school application process was complicated, but Amundsen was sort of my choice. Do you have any questions for me about high school? Are you scared? Nervous? Have you ever been to a concert?

Sincerely,
Samantha G.

Hello Samantha,

I like the introduction of yourself. Thank you for answering my questions. What career do you want to pursue? My dream job always changes, but at the moment I want to go to a culinary arts high school so I can maybe become a cook or chef.

My father is a chef and, whenever my family is in the kitchen, it's always the most fun. Since we (me, my mom, dad, and sister) all put our hands in the food, everyone helps do something and prepare dinner. Ever since I was in kindergarten, when my mom would start to cook dinner, I've always loved to help her peel and cut the fruit and vegetables. Then, when I was in fourth grade, I wanted to be a music therapist when I grew up because I wanted to help people who needed it—help clients improve their physical and mental health.

How was your first day in high school? Would you change anything you did on that first day? I am scared and nervous to meet new people, and to try to make friends. I have never gone to a concert, but I would love to go to one. Have you ever been to a concert? If so, how was it? Was it the best day of your life?

826CHI gave us writing prompts to choose from so here are mine:

1. *Think of a place or person that is special to you. Describe your subject using all of your senses.* I chose to write about my mom ♥.

Smell: When she comes home from work at 7 p.m. and I come near her, I smell the sweat that has been sitting on her body the whole day while she was working. It smells sweet.

Feel: I can feel the curls from my mom's black hair. It's trying to be all tamed into a ponytail.

See: I see my mom's birthmark on her nose and the many other moles on her neck. I love to touch them. I think she is beautiful. I can also see the wrinkles on the sides of her eyes when she smiles and laughs.

Hear: I hear the loud sips she takes while drinking her hot tea. I can also hear her complain to me that I didn't help out with all the chores, even though I always do!

Taste: When I kiss her cheek when she arrives home, it tastes like cold ice water which makes sense since it's winter outside.

2. *Write about the best day of your life.*
The best day of my life was when I was tall enough to get on the big roller coasters at Six Flags. I've always been really short. How tall are you? I'm just five feet tall. My sister and her fiance took me and my brother to Six Flags. My sister, Priscilla, and my brother, Damian, loved riding roller coasters, but my sister's fiancé, Miguel, was really scared to go on them. When we got in line for X-Flight I was starting to get nervous, but I was still so excited to get on and do a three-sixty. That was the part I was the most excited about. When it was finally our turn to get on, I sat with Damian. While I was riding on the roller coaster, all my nerves went away. My adrenaline overpowered them I guess. It was all so fun from the beginning till the end, but when the ride was over, I was not satisfied. I wanted to get on endless roller coasters! The Goliath, Batman, Superman, Vertical Velocity, Raging Bull—I want to ride them all. Do you like roller coasters?

3. *Free space! Write about whatever it is that you want. What's on your mind right now?*
I chose to write about the only dog I have ever owned. Me and my family have only owned one dog. Her name was Rapunzel. When I was in the fifth grade, I wanted a dog. After I finally convinced my mom, we went into dog

shelters to see prices. My mom would always say it was too expensive until one day when she came home with big news. She told us her coworker was giving some dogs away if we wanted one. When we went to check on the dogs, we all liked the same one. Her name was Piña. She had mixed colors: brown, white, and black. My mom hated the name Piña, so she decided she wanted the name of a princess. When she thought about it thoroughly, she decided on the name Rapunzel. No one disagreed with the name.

I would like to tell you that I can't wait to read your next letter!

Sincerely,
Alejandra Almaraz

Dear Alejandra,

Hello, writing these letters has made it easier to open up with another person. My dream job? Hmm, I actually have so many. I too would like to pursue a job or at least take an undergrad class in culinary arts. I love to cook and I absolutely love food. One other dream job would be a social worker. You know, the kind where a person lays down on a couch and speaks as the social worker sits in a chair and listens? My father is a chef too and he makes the most delicious food. Helping in the kitchen has become so natural for me. I love helping my mom in any way I can, just to help her take a load off after a long day of hard work.

Answering question time! Okay, so my first day in high school was super emotional because I was feeling like five hundred things at once. I was nervous about starting new and fresh, and worried if I'd make any friends. I was feeling excited because I love new beginnings and meeting people, even though I'm kind of semi-shy. I wouldn't change anything besides getting lost. Don't worry about the kids so much. Everyone in high school is completely obnoxious. You'll meet the greatest people ever and the worst. One thing, though: never lose who you truly are for another person or people. Even if they say they're your "friends." Another thing is to focus all your attention on your homework because you will fall behind SO FAST.

The concert I went to was for The Weeknd ♥. It was for my fifteenth birthday. It was amazing. It was for the Beauty Behind the Madness Tour. I was somewhere in the middle of the crowd. It was hot and dark and everyone was singing at the top of their lungs. The vibe was amazing and he sounds even better live.

For your next letter, I have a question: what does the word *hope* mean to you? Have you ever felt hopeful or hopeless? I have felt both. I have recently been feeling hopeless.

Sincerely,
Samantha

Dear Samantha,

In the beginning of your last letter you wrote, "Writing these letters has made it easier to open up with another person," and I totally agree with you. I have told you many things about who I am as a person and about my identity. Yet, usually when I meet a person (for the first time), I tend to get extremely shy and will barely talk. The vibe between me and the person begins to get awkward. Yet every time I have written these letters to you, I not have felt awkward. Such a disappointment that we have to discontinue these back and forth letters! It was an amazing experience for me. Was it for you?

The visual I got while reading your answers to my questions about high school was full hallways and many, many, many stairs that I WILL get lost in, very easily. If I got lost, I would be extremely shy to ask anyone for help. Which sucks. LOL.

:O I am surprised you also like culinary arts and that your dad is a chef. That's so cool.

What has been the reason you have lately been feeling hopeless? Personally, I have felt hopeless before. The thing that kept me from losing all my hope was my mom. Me and my mom were going through something, and yet my mom was always acting calm toward the subject. She never cried. (Well, at least not in front of me.) She always kept a serious, normal, and happy profile. I wanted to follow her steps and did the same as her.

Advice I would love to give you: when you feel hopeless, it may be better for you if you tell a close friend. Maybe this person can relate to exactly what you are going through. I suggest that you hang out with people who only give good vibes. Probably when you see their calmness towards the thing you are sad about, you will slowly begin to gain your hope.

Sincerely,
Alejandra

Dear Alejandra,

Hey :). I'm glad you agree with me. I like to get to know people, but sometimes my shyness prevents it. Or, my resting mean mugface makes people afraid to come up to me. I have also told you things about how I am feeling, what I think, and even about my past. It is a disappointment that these letters have to come to an end. I did enjoy this experience very much :). Don't worry, tons of kids get lost on their first day. Don't be shy to ask for help.

Well, it's kind of dumb why I have been feeling down. My ex-boyfriend of ten months dumped me, then started dating a new girl a week later. I was really depressed for a very long time. I'm still a little bit sad but, you know, trying to get over it. My mom is actually one of the few people who helped me in this very low point. I tell her everything. Our relationship wasn't always like this, but I am super glad it is now. My mom bought me so much food to make me feel better. I even dyed my hair. LOL. New me, I guess.

Thank you for the advice ♥. I was having a very tough day and honestly, I was about to break down. I went to my counselor and that helped a lot ♥.

Sincerely,
Sam Gutierrez ♥

P.S. I wish you the best in life and in high school ♥.

SAMANTHA GUTIERREZ is sixteen years old and attends Amundsen High School. Her favorite time of year is fall, when you can wear shorts and a hoodie. Her pride and joy is her dog. She is also a complete bookworm and a Harry Potter freak. When she grows up she wants to go to college and become successful. She wants to travel the world to help those who cannot help themselves. She is someone who turns a bad moment into a great one. Weird fact: baby carrots and apple sauce taste good together.

ALEJANDRA ALMARAZ is a fourteen-year-old who lives in Chicago's Little Village. She attends Emiliano Zapata Academy and plans to attend World Language High School. She takes a five-hour nap every day. She is not a morning person, but a night person. She is always laughing. When her face turns red some people call her *Tomate*. She is the youngest sister. Her height is four-foot-eleven. She will be a college graduate.

I AM:

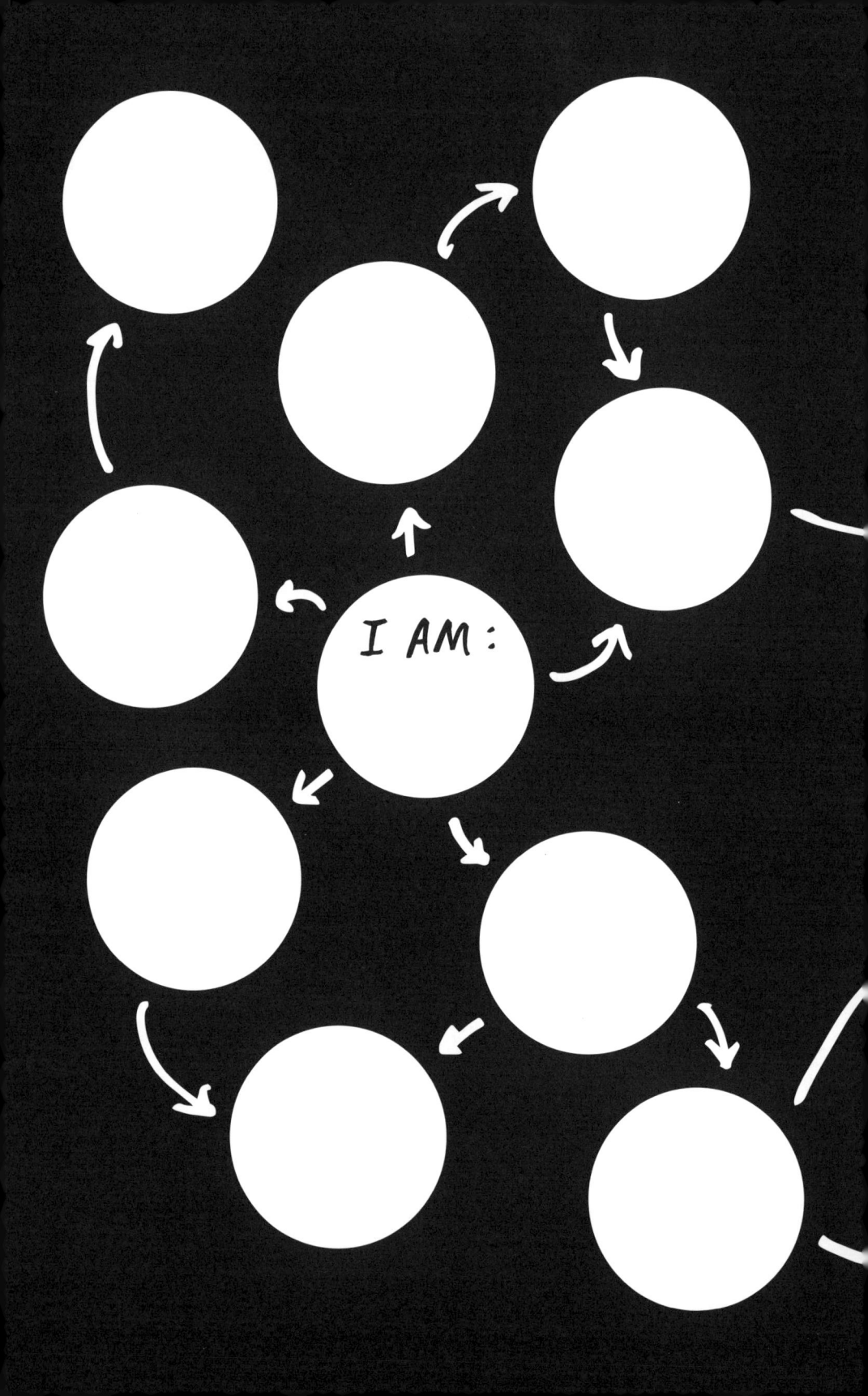

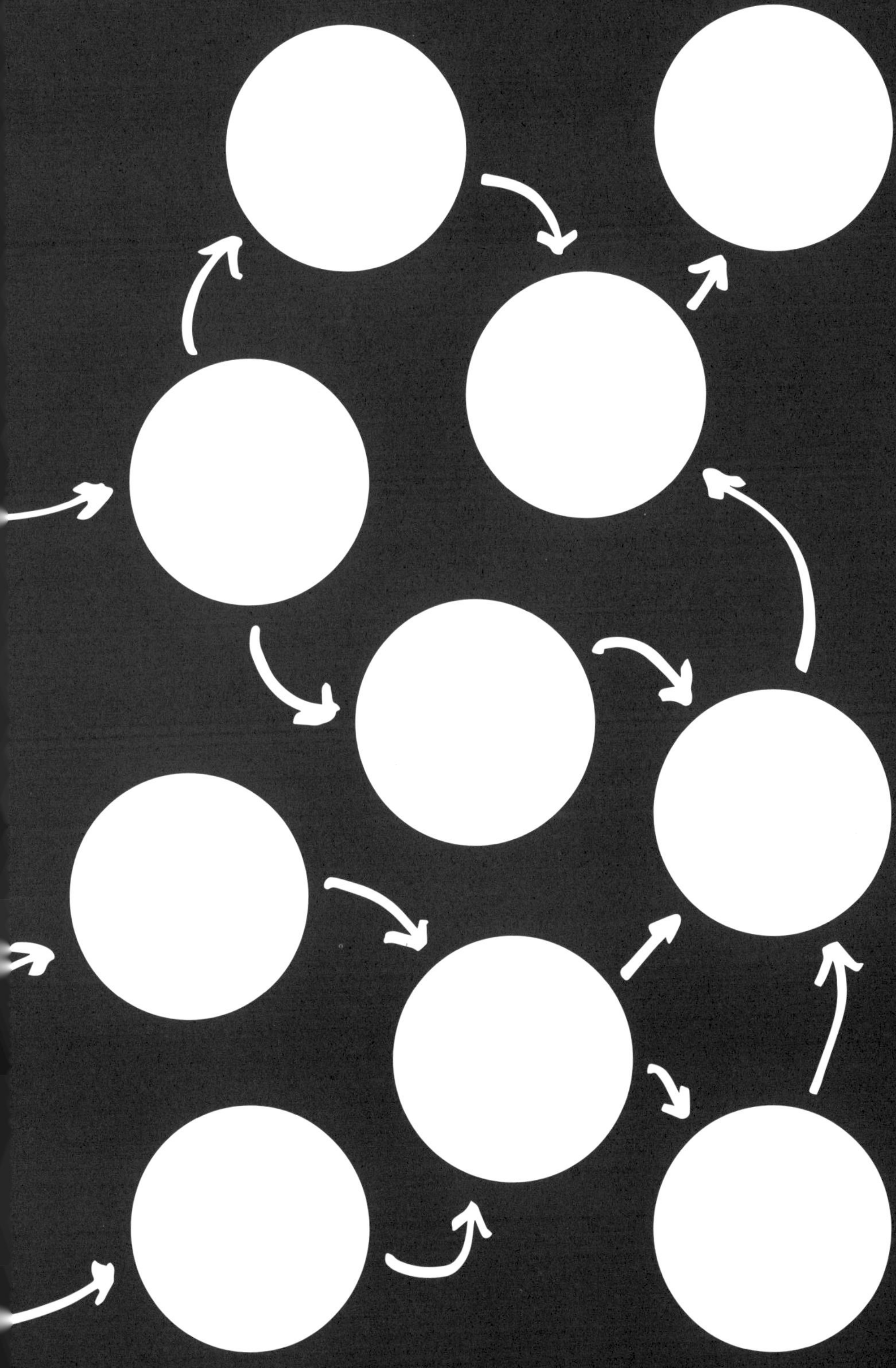

FAAIZ SHAKIL & JENNIFER MOCTEZUMA

Dear Faaiz,

I hope you had a great Thanksgiving! One of my favorite things to do is to read, and I have a favorite book I wanted to recommend to you. It's called *House Arrest* by K.A. Holt. I think it's a good book.

I have some questions for you. Do you like or watch anime? I love anime. I remember the first anime I watched was *Naruto* and that was when I was seven, but my favorite anime is *Black Butler*. What kind of games do you play? Do you have any brothers or sisters? What's the last movie you saw?

The last movie I saw was *Finding Dory* and I actually started crying when I was watching it. If you have not watched it, watch it! What's your favorite subject? Mine is a tie! It's either reading or social studies. Lately, we have been learning about the Holocaust, which is my favorite topic. But I also like reading, because books! Yeah, it's a tie.

Well, I hope you have a great day! Talk to you soon.

Sincerely,
Jennifer M.

P.S. You see that drawing? Well, he does not have a name. What do you think I should name him?

Dear Jennifer,

I like the drawing you made, but I don't have a name for it yet. It's really hard choosing a name.

The last movie I watched was *Guardians of the Galaxy*. I know it's been awhile since the movie came out, but at the time I thought it was going to be like a bad copy of *Star Wars* so I didn't see it. I was wrong, it was awesome.

Some other things about me: I am fifteen years old. I was born in Pakistan and came to Chicago when I was four. I actually haven't traveled to any other part of America since. I have three siblings: an older brother, a younger sister, and a younger brother. So, I'm like the middle child. Do you have any siblings? I would say that my younger siblings get the most attention because my younger brother, well he's only five, so that's one reason for him. My sister is the only girl sibling, so my parents give her attention too. When it's her birthday, my parents throw a big party and invite all of her friends.

The types of games I like to play are action-packed games like *Call of Duty*. I also play *NBA 2K*, but that's the only sports game I like. I try to play basketball in real life, but I'm not that good. Basketball is the only sport I like to play. A few other questions I have for you are: what are some things you are interested in and what's something recent that happened to you that was fun? I hope you have a great day!

Sincerely,
Faaiz Shakil

P.S. I watched *Finding Dory* and you're right, it was a great movie.

"Lately, I have been interested in politics but not really that much. Like I can only talk about it a little bit because then I get really bored."

Dear Faaiz,

I enjoyed reading your letter, especially when you started talking about where you came from. Lately, I have been interested in politics but not really that much. Like I can only talk about it a little bit because then I get really bored. Other than politics, I'm really interested in animation. My number one job I want to do is animation, like creating or animating a cartoon.

I'm going to ask you only five questions since this is the last letter I will be sending to you. First question: Do you do any after school activities? Like, I'm in homework club. What three jobs do you want to do? Okay, I know I said that I was going to ask you five questions, but my head is out of questions.

But (butts) I did want to ask you if you had a name for the little drawing I made. I know it's hard coming up with a name, but hopefully you have one and you will tell me in your last letter!

Well, Faaiz, this is the end of my letter.

Sincerely,
Jennifer

P.S. I can't wait to meet you!

Dear Jennifer,

I am glad you liked my letter. I really thought your letter was cool too.

I have the same feeling about politics. I can talk about it for a little, but after a while it gets boring. I don't really have an after school activity, but I am thinking about joining this program where they help you get prepared for college. Some jobs that I would like to do are game designing, writing, or being an artist. I would choose these jobs because they are all creative.

I want to tell you something about myself. At this age, I have done a lot of crazy things. I broke my leg for the first time. Not only that, but a lot of other crazy things have happened too.

Okay, this is all I have to say in this letter. I hope to see you soon.

Sincerely,
Faaiz

P.S. I think the drawing's name should be Tie Guy.

FAAIZ SHAKIL is a sophomore at Amundsen High School. He enjoys comedy movies and action movies, too. He loves to eat all junk foods. He's a middle child in his family. When he was young, he went to Pakistan to visit relatives. He speaks Urdu. He also loves playing video games. He really likes FPS (first-person shooter) games and action games. He doesn't really have a favorite class, but he's taking swimming lessons and that's pretty fun.

JENNIFER MOCTEZUMA is a fourteen-year-old who goes to Zapata Academy. She loves to draw and paint. She also likes to read almost any type of book and loves to hear conspiracy theories. She was an only child but is now a sister. She will be an animator, a writer, and an artist. She will be the very best!

ALEXA SOTO & CITHLALY BETHANCOURT

Dear Alexa,

Hi!! I'm Cithlaly, an eighth grader at Zapata Academy. I have two sisters, a little sister and an older sister. My little sister is different. For example, she likes to hang out with guys rather than girls. Now, my older sister, she has Down Syndrome. I know it's hard to process that, but I don't want you to treat me differently. I love creating and hearing music. I am Mexican American, so I love tacos. By the way, you can call me Laly, everybody does.

I truly enjoyed reading your survey and learning a little bit of who you are. I felt a great connection with you just by reading your survey! For example: hair. I'm guessing you have wavy or straight hair? Well, I have curly hair. I love it but hate it at the same time! You can't do anything with it, well at least not that I know of! Got any suggestions for how to do curly hair?

Well anyway, I'm truly looking forward to knowing more about you. How was your freshman year? What kinds of tips would you give an eighth grader (like me!) who is starting their freshman year next year? What is your favorite childhood memory? Do you have any siblings? Who is your fave celebrity? Who inspires you to be the person you are today? I hope we get to know more about you as time flies! And I can't wait to read your letter.

With love,
Cithlaly Betancourt

P.S. Eighth grade is really (surprisingly!) going well! In seventh grade, I was scared to do something wrong that would affect me, but hey, I'm here! And I prefer The Fault in Our Stars as the movie. It's easier to make a story in my mind, rather than reading the book.

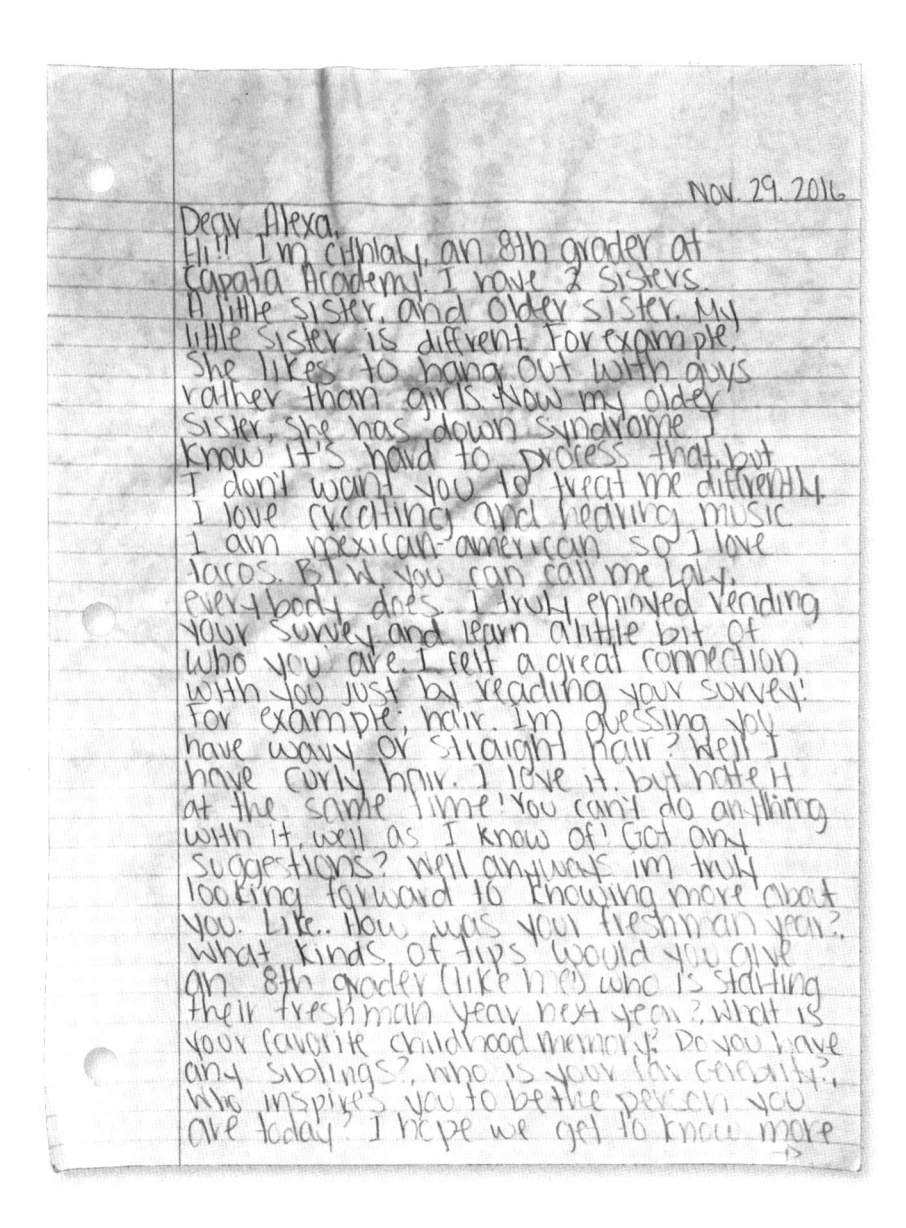

Nov. 29, 2016

Dear Alexa,

Hi!! I'm Cithlaly, an 8th grader at Capata Academy! I have 2 sisters. A little sister, and older sister. My little sister is diffrent for example! She likes to hang out with guys rather than girls. Now my older sister, she has down syndrome. I know it's hard to process that, but I don't want you to treat me differently. I love exercising and hearing music. I am mexican-american so I love tacos. BTW you can call me Laly, everybody does. I truly enjoyed reading your survey and learn a little bit of who you are. I felt a great connection with you just by reading your survey! For example; hair. I'm guessing you have wavy or straight hair? Well I have curly hair. I love it, but hate it at the same time! You can't do anything with it, well as I know of! Got any suggestions? Well anyways im truly looking forward to knowing more about you. Like.. How was your freshman year? What kinds of tips would you give an 8th grader (like me) who is starting their freshman year next year?, What is your favorite childhood memory? Do you have any siblings?, Who is your fav. celebrity?, Who inspires you to be the person you are today? I hope we get to know more →

Dear Laly,

Hey! My name is Alexa, but I'm guessing you already that. I actually have two sisters too. My younger sister is only eight years old and my older sister is twenty going on twenty-one. I really enjoy listening to Twenty One Pilots and PTX (Pentatonix). I'll actually listen to any type of music except country. I don't really create music like you do, but I do like tampering with songs, like making mashups of already-created songs.

I'm Mexican American like you, but for some reason I'm better at making Asian foods like egg rolls and rangoons. I do have straight hair. I usually braid it before I go to sleep in order for it to look nice in the morning. For you, I suggest doing what my friend Miyann does and just leave it curly the way it is, but put in some coconut oil for the frizz. It looks really nice that way. Some suggestions for high school: just stay on top of your grades and out of drama. (Trust me, it's not worth it.)

My fave childhood memory is going to Disney in L.A. with my parents when I was seven, which was fun. My favorite celeb is Mitch Grassi (who is in Superfruit on YouTube) and in PTX. I honestly just love him so much.

What about you? What's your favorite kind of music? Who's your favorite celeb? What's your favorite kind of food? What's your favorite sport? I look forward to talking to you more.

Sincerely,
Alexa

Hey Alexa ♥,

I was super excited that I got to receive a letter back from you!! It was really weird to realize that we have a lot in common. Even my classmate Marco thought that it was "pretty strange but cool"! The first thing that we have in common is how we're both stuck in the middle of our sisters!

My younger sister Ayline and I have gone through so many things together. Some of those memories were funny or sad, and others uncomfortable. There was this one time when my mom, my sister, and I were at Target in the laundry detergent aisle. Well, my crazy coupon lady mother decided to make us find a certain type of detergent that she wanted. Now, my mother is not to be messed with, so we were kind of forced to find it! While my mom was on her phone looking for more coupons, my sister and I saw a puddle of blue detergent on the floor of the aisle. Obviously, we went around it to try and avoid falling. My mom didn't, though. She stepped right onto the detergent, slipped, and fell! It was hilarious! We couldn't stop laughing! This moment was one of those memories that you will forever remember. (By the way, my mom got so mad at us for not telling her about the puddle that she didn't want to talk to us for the rest of the day!) Anyway, do you have any memories with your family? What about your sisters?

What is your favorite memory, or best day of your life? So, my best day of my life was when I was around eleven. I was vacationing with my family. We were at Disney World at Magic Kingdom! It was super fun to get on the rides and just to be there, but my favorite part was toward the end. Before the goodbye celebration, there was a light show. It was the end of July so it was super hot, and when it got super dark all the characters came out and started to do their parade around the whole park.

Now, are you ready for my favorite part? Okay, so everybody gathered around the Princess Castle and the fireworks started to go. *Boom, boom, boom!* They were different colors and super pretty! All of the characters voices came in over the speakers, saying their famous quotes. At the end, Mickey Mouse's voice came out. He said, "We'll see you soon!" It was such an awesome memory because it was my first time there and being able to see the Princess Castle. All of my childhood characters in real life just made me feel like I was home, safe and secure. Have you ever felt like that? What kind of relationship do you and your parents have?

I'm so sad that I have to say bye, but I will be waiting for your next letter ♥!

With love,
Cithlaly ♥

P.S. I also don't like country music, but I can work with anything else!

Hi Cithlaly!

It's crazy how much we have in common! My mom is also a crazy coupon lady. She'll make us waste thirty minutes out of each Sunday to help her cut out coupons. It's pretty boring.

I do have a lot of memories with my family. We play around a lot with each other and even play fight sometimes. It's fun. The memory that sticks out to me most was probably when we took a three-day trip to Wisconsin. We were staying in a cabin in the middle of the woods which seems scary but is actually pretty fun. We spent the morning climbing up a huge hill that had a ski lift at the top. Obviously it was turned off since we were there in the middle of summer.

Anyway, I decided it would be a good idea to go explore the tall grass with my cousin Danna and my dad. My dad found a nest with pretty big eggs in it. He took a bunch of pictures and left to go show my mom. My cousin and I got closer to the nest to see the eggs a bit better. We were about two feet away when a huge turkey started running toward us. We got scared, screamed, and sprinted through the thorns and sticks until I tripped over an overgrown branch. It seemed pretty terrifying at the moment but is overall a hilarious memory. So, yeah, my family and I are pretty close. We have loads of great memories.

My greatest memory, honestly, has to be the day I went to my first Pentatonix concert. It was on a school day (Thursday) so as you can imagine I was pretty hyped up waiting until 3 p.m. I had two tickets: one was for me and the other was originally for my dad, but he was nice enough to let my boyfriend go with me. It was a pretty long drive to the Allstate Arena and the line was UNBELIEVABLE, but it was worth the wait and totally worth getting there two hours early. I got to stand in the very front with my boyfriend. We were about two feet away from the stage! They sang all my favorite songs, and I even got to touch Mitch! (It's a pretty big deal to me—I'm obsessed.) I was super tired after all the screaming and jumping, but it definitely is my best memory.

Have you ever been to a concert? Who's your favorite musician? What's the best memory you've had with music? Anyway, I've got to go. Can't wait to read your next letter!

Alexa ♥

Dear Alexa,

I want to say thank you! It's been such a great time being able to write to you. I really appreciate all of your effort that I feel through reading your letters. I am beyond excited to meet you! I literally can't wait for that day ♥.

Anyway, I want to talk (or write!) about such an important person in my life. This human being passed away a couple of years ago, but the memories haven't gone. I was around seven years old. I was at my grandma's house, playing on the swings. Then, a couple of pigeons appeared and I basically tried to scare them away. While doing that, I decided to walk backwards. When (I thought) I got to the swing, I sat down, but it was not the swing, it was a CACTUS! It was a horrible feeling to sit on a cactus but also very funny. When I told my grandma about it after, she couldn't stop laughing. It was probably one of the best memories that I have with her. Her death really impacted me. Have you ever had someone that you care a lot for suddenly leave you?

My grandma also helped me find one of my biggest passions—music. Talking about music: my favorite musicians are Michael Jackson, Ariana Grande, Banda MS, and CNCO ♥. Best experiences with music? I got to sing with *mariachis* at my church for La Virgen de Guadalupe. You make remixes, right? Well, do you want to be in some way involved with music in your future?

It's been such a pleasure to write with you, Alexa. Be proud of who you are and don't forget that. No matter who you are, what you do, or where you are from, you should ALWAYS love yourself and be proud of who you are. Thank you once again ♥. See you in June!

Laly ♥

ALEXA SOTO is fifteen years old. She's a musician who plays the flute and the piano. She loves to write short stories and poems. Alexa's favorite musical group is Pentatonix, and her favorite singer is Mitch Grassi. She loves horror movies and *The Walking Dead*. She loves video games, food, and Mitch Grassi (yeah, again).

CITHALY BETANCOURT is fourteen years old. She loves to discover new things and meet new people. She is basically an adventurer. Even though she used to overthink and be self-conscious all the time, she wants to be a leader, an inspiration, and a person who others can look up to. Cithaly also wants to travel the world, specifically to Brazil and Europe. She does not worry about guy problems or relationships, which her dad thinks is great! Cithaly also gets very stressed out when she gets a C in her grades. Her main focus is succeeding in life for her parents. Even though she might be serious at times, deep down in her heart she is a goofy child who will never grow up.

"My favorite food is my mom's."

DAVID POP &
DANIEL NAVARRETE

Dear David,

Hello, my name is Daniel, but I like to be called Danny. I'm from Chicago, but my family came from Mexico. I have one brother, one younger sister, and one older sister. Do you have any siblings and are you close with them? My favorite sport right now is volleyball, how about you? My favorite food is my mom's. It's the best. Do you have a favorite place to eat? My favorite place to eat is Panda Express because I love Chinese food.

I saw on the survey that you like to play video games. What games do you play on your PS4? I love *Call of Duty*—how about you? Do you play extended hours?

Do you enjoy school? What is there to enjoy about it? Did you have any struggles in freshman year? You also mentioned you like MLG? What do you watch and what's your favorite competitive team?

Well, I hope you have a good week.

Sincerely,
Danny

Dear Danny,

What's up? That's cool that you're from Mexico. I am from Romania. School is actually pretty fun because you have a lot more freedom, but you also have a lot of responsibilities. My freshman year was good, but now I regret not trying my hardest.

I mostly like PC gaming now because I just finished building my PC last week. I used only high-end parts, so I spent a lot of money on it. It took me around two days to finish building it. I mostly play *CS:GO* and *Rainbow Six Siege*.

I remember every moment from when I broke my arm. I was four years old. My family and I were getting ready to go to my cousin's house. Me and my brother got dressed quickly, and we went down stairs to blast some music. I kept running across the couches and at the end of the couch, I would jump over a chair and land on some pillows. In one moment, I forgot to jump so I tripped over the chair. On the wall there was a really big coat hanger that I tried to grab onto so I wouldn't fall. I almost held onto it, but my hand slipped! I landed on my elbow and it automatically came out the other side. I started crying because of the pain, so my brother ran upstairs fast to tell my parents what had happened. My parents rushed downstairs. When my mom saw me she actually fainted. I arrived at the hospital and they rushed me to the surgery room. After that, I remember waking up and seeing my family and my cousin's family, and that made me so happy that I cried. I was in the hospital for a couple of weeks. I played with other kids from the hospital. This was probably the scariest thing that has happened to me.

What are some scary moments you've had? Have you ever been hospitalized? Hope you have a good week.

Sincerely,
David

Dear David,

How have you been? Thank you for the letter. I also built a PC in the summer and my dad helped me. I enjoyed building the computer. Did anyone help you build your PC? What are any responsibilities you have at school? Are your responsibilities important to you?

One scary moment I had was when a couple of friends and I walked along the playground. We were just walking when two teachers called my name, and I didn't know they had called my name! The teachers told me that I had cursed at them from a distance, but I never did. They sent me to go talk to our assistant principal. He told me about the teachers' complaint and that I had denied it. I told him that we were just walking until I was called by the teachers. Mr. Ramirez, our assistant principal, told me that he could tell I was being honest and that I didn't do anything wrong, so he let me go.

Has something ever happened to you like this? Were you confused and scared like I was? I look forward to meeting you in person. Oh, and I hope you have a really good week and enjoy yourself.

Sincerely,
Danny

Dear Danny,

Something like that hasn't really happened to me, but once I got blamed for stealing something, which I never did. It got me very mad and scared because they called the cops. They came and they started blaming me, but I kept telling them that I didn't do it. We kept arguing and then I realized there was a security camera, so I told the police officer to look at the footage. He didn't really want to look at it because he was really mad and frustrated, so I kept getting louder and louder until they put me in the car. The police called my parents. When my parents showed up. they started talking. I told my dad to ask for the camera footage, so they finally took a look at it. After they saw it, they realized that it wasn't me. They apologized and they let me go. This was a pretty scary moment from my life. See you soon!

Sincerely,
David

DAVID POP is Romanian, and he's sixteen years old. He goes to Amundsen and he loves working with computers. A cool fact about him is that he goes fishing very often. While he goes ocean fishing if it's a nice day, he also goes scuba diving. He loves scuba diving because he gets to explore a lot. He plays lacrosse for a team in Skokie and he's a defender. He started playing lacrosse in 2016.

DANIEL NAVARRETE is a fourteen-year-old boy who enjoys music, loves video games, and hates half of everything. Daniel was born in Chicago and has lived here all his life. Daniel wants to be something, but hasn't decided what yet. Daniel believes that anyone can be whatever they put their mind to.

"Do you have a crush? I have a crush, but he is famous."

YOU! & RUTH AGUILERA

EDITOR'S NOTE: *Ruth's letter-writing partner transferred schools mid-year and, sadly, we are no longer in touch with her. Bonus writing prompt for you, dear reader: Pretend to be Ruth's letter-writing partner by ghostwriting the missing responses!*

Dear new friend,

My name is Ruth Aguilera and I'm Mexican. I am thirteen years old. I was born in Mexico and, lucky for me, I have all my family with me. They all love to eat anything you give them. I've been in Zapata schools since I was three years old.

What do you dream of doing when you grow up? I would love to be a doctor because I want to learn about new stuff, different diseases. Let me tell you, I love music and my favorite song would have to be "Starboy" by The Weeknd. I love that song. What music do you like?

How old are you? What race are you? When is your birthday? How did it go in your freshman year? Do you play any sports? Do you have a crush? I have a crush, but he is famous. His name is Jacob Sartorius. He is fourteen years old, and he is a singer and a model. He is like the cutest thing ever.

Hopefully we get to be friends on social media. I can't wait to meet you face-to-face.

Sincerely,
Ruth Aguilera

DEAR RUTH,

Dear friend,

I really loved the way you wrote me a letter back. I think it's really amazing what you want to do when you grow up because so far, from all my classmates, none of them want to do that. It's sad that you don't have a crush on no one, but you will find someone better. And yeah, you may think that I'm too young to have a crush, but believe it or not, many girls in this school have boyfriends.

I have some more questions for you. Do you speak Spanish? What advice could you give me for high school? Has anyone bullied you?

I'm really glad I'm gonna be able to call you my friend ♥ ♥.

Sincerely,
Ruth Aguilera

P.S (You seem Really cool And I cant wait!)

DEAR RUTH,

YOU: _____

RUTH AGUILERA is a fourteen-year-old who lives in Chicago. Her favorite food is *tamales*. She wants to travel the whole world and likes to make people laugh. She is the oldest sister in her family. If she only had three wishes she would wish for freedom, no rules, and for it to always be summer. Ruth wants to be a doctor when she grows up. She wants to have her own building with her name in big letters on it.

ISABELLA RODRIGUEZ & JORGE SUAREZ

Dear Isabella,

My name is Jorge Suarez and what I like to do is play soccer, either after school or on the weekends. I also like playing volleyball with my brother and his friends. The high school I would like to go to is either Infinity or Curie. My brother has told me a lot about Infinity's sports teams for volleyball and soccer.

Do you have any high school experiences you can tell me about? What do you like to do after school? Do you play any sports?

Sincerely,
Jorge Suarez

Dear Jorge,

I go to Amundsen High School and it's a very diverse school. I'm not in as many sports as before. I used to be on the cheerleading team at my high school. In my personal life, I do MMA. In case you don't know, MMA is all different types of martial arts. I started doing MMA because my mom was in Aikido and she's a black belt. I believe I've been doing MMA for six and a half years. Do you like any other types of sports? The reason I'm not doing my athletic activities anymore is because I'm in Advanced Band and am focusing on that in particular since it takes up a lot of my time. I play the flute.

Do you like hockey? The Blackhawks are my favorite team! For soccer, do you like Chivas or América? Currently in my life, I'm thinking of taking some dance classes. Either ballet, hip-hop, K-pop, or just creating my own dance club in general.

Sincerely,
Isabella Chiara Rodriguez Petrov

Dear Isabella

So you've done mma for almost 7 years are you like a profesional at mma? I do like hockey I just dont watch hockey as much as soccer and I dont really like playing hockey either Because I get hit alot in the legs. I am a Chivas Fan and I do not like america they lost the Final By the way. do you have any Brothers or sister that steal your chargers or any other things from you? In my neighborhood at 7am is quite and normal but 7pm it's dark outside and the street ligths dont work and you can hear fast cars flying Because they go to fast on speed Bumps.

     Sincerly
     Jorge Suarez

Dear Isabella,

You've done MMA for almost seven years—are you like a professional? I do like hockey, but I don't watch it as much as soccer. I don't really like playing hockey, either, because I get hit a lot in the legs. I am a Chivas fan and I do not like América because they lost in the final.

In my neighborhood at 7 a.m. it is quiet and normal. But at 7 p.m. it's dark outside, the street lights don't work, and you can hear cars firing because they go too fast on speed bumps. Where I live, there is also lots of killing. Last year a mom got shot by her husband. There was also a kidnapping right in front of my house. They went into our yard to hide so the police asked us if we knew anything, but we didn't.

How's high school going? There really isn't drama here except for some break-ups and a few girls not being friends anymore. By the way, do you have any brothers or sisters who steal your chargers or any other things from you?

Sincerely,
Jorge

P.S. What's your favorite candy? What are you going to do this summer?

Dear Jorge,

Well, I love all candy except Snickers. I don't like nuts, so that's why. I wouldn't call myself a *professional* at MMA since I haven't gone to any competitions yet, but I do spar with my friends at the academy. When I play hockey, my fingers are usually what gets hit going after the puck. I guess you could say I'm an América fan by association since almost all of my family likes América. Ironically, my best friend and her family are Chivas fans (minus her uncle).

I have one sister who is always taking stuff from my mom and me. Luckily, she has an iPhone and I have a Samsung, so she has absolutely no use for my chargers :). My neighborhood is pretty noisy. I always hear sirens, fireworks, gunshots, speeding cars, and all kinds of people yelling. But then again, I live right next to an alley.

This summer, my best friend and I are going to be applying to go on a trip to Japan. I'm also going to redecorate my room because I'm in need of a change. My room was last painted when I was three, so I've had a pink room for twelve years! I'm going to repaint it with my *lovelies* (that's what I call my best friends). We're each going to make a unique mural that connects to who we are and who we want to be. Also, my family and I are going to try a healthier lifestyle. I'm going to grow out my hair and dye it. I also want to get some tattoos, whenever that's possible. The reasoning for all my changes is because I'm been trying to find myself under my own standards. I've been confused about some things lately.

In all honesty, I am not that open with people unless I feel comfortable with them, but I can say that lately I've been lost in my thoughts, questioning so many things. I refuse to even tell my friends at school because recently they've been talking about what I told them with their other friends. The only topic any of my friends have been talking about are relationships and cheating. One of my guy friends has been lecturing me because this guy I like has a reputation for dating multiple girls at a time and then breaking up with them once he's slept with them! I defended my crush though, because I feel bad that he had a horrible childhood and that's not his fault. My friends are all saying that he is just acting.

I'm sorry for laying all this info on you. It's just that everyone is being very frustrating, getting into my business when I never even said that I was going to date that guy! All I said was that he's cute and that I can sympathize with him. I apologize for possibly being way too open for you to handle =D. I hope your life is going easier than mine.

Sincerely, for a final good-bye,
Isabella Chiara Rodriguez Petrov

ISABELLA RODRIGUEZ is fifteen years old and she goes to Amundsen High School. She used to suffer from depression, but now she is more artistic, joyous, and friendly. She would like to be more open and travel the world with her best friends. A lot of the time she's very closed-up until she becomes more comfortable with the people she is surrounded by. She quit mixed martial arts in order to discover herself since all she knew was MMA for over six years, and she didn't feel very feminine. Since quitting MMA, she has discovered more interests like her new love of nail art and learning new hairstyles. She describes herself as a dreamer, artistic, and happy-go-lucky. Occasionally, yes, she is somewhat dark or mean . . . but she doesn't want to show that side of herself unless it comes out because she's defending herself.

JORGE SUAREZ is a thirteen-year-old who goes to Zapata Academy. He lives in Chicago and likes to play soccer, but also enjoys buying junk food. He likes to play *Call of Duty: Black Ops 2* and tries to stay out of trouble. He wants to be a soccer player when he grows up.

ANGELES NIETO & JULIETA LARA

Dear Angeles Nieto,

Hey! How are you doing? How's the high school life? I guess I'll introduce myself now. My name is Julieta Lara and I'm thirteen years old, about to turn fourteen on December 7. So what are some things I should know about you? Some things you should know about me are:

- I was in debate and I hope to continue it in high school.
- I like to read webtoons and comics.
- I watch way too much television.
- I watch tons of anime.
- I LOVE K-pop.
- I draw a lot.
- I have tons of bad luck in gym (like not hitting the ball and hitting the ball with my face *sigh*).
- I'm gender-neutral but prefer the male look rather than female look.

I told you my gender identity because I want you to be curious about different identities. I'm a bit confused on whether you're male or female because Angeles is a boy's name, but you also mentioned Angie.

Also, here are some other questions that I wanted to ask you: what do you hope to do after high school? Also, if you take trains, buses, or other modes of transportation to school, how did you know which streets, buses, or trains to take?

I can say that getting into a good high school is one of my main priorities. The high school I really want to get into is Lane Tech College Prep. I really love it! What type of personality do you have? I'm positive, outgoing, optimistic, and loyal. Okay, I think this is long enough. I'll just wait for your response. Sorry for the messy handwriting. I'm rushing this. I only have two minutes left, AHH! Hope you have a nice day and that you had a nice Thanksgiving! To be honest, this is how my handwriting really looks.

Love,
Julieta Lara

ew that looks horrible...

Dear Julieta Zara,

Hi! I'm doing pretty decent. I'm sixteen years old—I just turned sixteen on October 10. I'm a female by the way, HA! I think my name is pretty unique. I've never met someone of heard someone with my name.

Some things you should know about me: I'm the whole opposite of you, based on what what you've told me! I can't watch TV because I always end up falling asleep after ten minutes. I used to draw back in sixth grade, but now I suck.

After high school, I'm planning on going to college, but I don't know what I want to do. As for my personality, I'm pretty shy at the beginning, but once you get to know me I'm loud and crazy. I'm loving too. I care a lot about my family and close friends. I see that you're into many things and all I'm into is dancing, ha! Latino dancing is something I love. It's my passion!

Love,
Angie ♥
(Angeles N.)

Dear Angeles (Angie),

Hey! Just got your letter today! After I opened your letter, it gave me so much good luck. In PE, I could actually hit the ball and I wasn't too slow. My handwriting in my first letter was a bit messy because we had only two minutes left and we were already leaving for gym. I know my L's can sometimes look like Z's because I write H-O-R-R-I-B-L-E. My name is actually Julieta Lara, not Zara. Sorry to confuse you! Although, Zara sounds really cool.

Like you, I don't talk much at first, but once I've befriended someone I can get pretty loud. Also, what do you mean you fall asleep after ten minutes of TV?! If you sleep after just ten minutes then it might be for one of two reasons: either the shows aren't interesting or you're really sleepy, which means you don't get enough sleep. If you can't sleep on your own, try sleeping pills. I take sleeping pills because, if I don't, I don't fall asleep until 2 or 3 a.m.

I draw anime and realistic drawings, mainly eyes or anime faces. For some reason, I can't draw in pencil. Only in pen! Weird, right? There are only a few times when my eyes have come out nicely in pencil. I'll show you. Honestly, I've drawn eyes so many times, I can do all this in under a minute.

Oh hey, guess what? I made fourth place in the science fair! I was really surprised since I thought I'd totally fail, but I guess not!

Sincerely,
Julieta Lara

Dear Angie,

All right, I forgot to ask questions, so I'll send you this letter in two pieces. I'm sick :(. My head hurts, my neck hurts, and my throat hurts. Why am I even at school today? *Throws papers* Bye. Just kidding.

Today we got this tic-tac-toe paper where we answer three questions in a story format. So, let's get started with one, shall we?

I've talked to you about my art, books, and some other stuff, but I haven't told you any of my stories. The best day of my life was when I went to my first Debate tournament. I mean, sure, I was a nervous wreck, but I was also excited because I was going up against high schoolers and we were only in the seventh grade. Also, it was my first time staying out late, until like 7 or 8 p.m. I only got to do two rounds, but it was awesome. The debate coach left so we don't have debate now, but when I get to high school I want to join their debate team.

I also have some groups and songs that I would like to recommend to you:

Boy groups
- BTS - Save me
- BTS - Dope
- BTS - Blood, sweat, and tears
- BTS - War of hormones
- Bigbang - Bang Bang Bang
- Bigbang - last dance
- Bigbang - F××k it ← (Like that)
- Exo - Lotto
- Exo - monster
- Seventeen - nice

Girl groups
- Twice - cheer up
- Sonamoo - I really love you
- Blackpink - playing with fire
- Blackpink - whistle
- Blackpink - Boombayah

★ Jay park - aquaman

252

Solo artist   Jay park — put em' up
CL - Hello Bixches (actual curse word)
Taeyang - eyes, nose, lips
G dragon - Crooked
G dragon - good boy

You don't have to listen to all of these, but they are a bunch of songs that are pretty good. Please note that the only song in English is the one that I starred.

What college are you planning to go to? I want to go to a college that's really good with law since I want to be a lawyer. What's your dream job? Do you know what you want to major in? Are you gonna celebrate Christmas? I am. We're gonna open our presents at midnight on December 24. Hope you have a nice Christmas if you are celebrating!

Sincerely,
Julieta Lara

Dear Julieta Lara,

Hey! How have you been? I've been great other than the fact that my older sister has moved in. AHH! She's been sleeping in my room with her daughter.

Have you guys started high school applications yet? Also, I'm glad my letter gave you so much luck during gym! My Christmas and New Year's was boring. I got to spend Christmas with my dad's side and New Year's with my mom's, but I guess I didn't have any type of holiday spirit this year.

I was wondering, what is your race? That's always my first question while getting to know someone. I guess I can go from there into a deeper conversation. Any languages you know or speak other than English? Tell me more about your family.

I loved your drawings by the way! I'm only good at stick figures, ha! Well, hope to hear from you soon!

Sincerely,
Angeles Nieto

Dear Angeles,

I'm great! I'm hungry. We started applying to high schools on October 9. I applied to seven schools. So far, I've gotten accepted into Infinity High School and Chicago Tech High School.

My race? I'm Hispanic. My parents are Mexican, but I was born here in America. I know a lot of languages, but I only know a few words in each one. The languages I know are: English, Spanish, French, Korean, Japanese, and German. That's it, I think. How many languages do you know?

Also, about my family: we don't talk much and we don't go on family vacations all together.

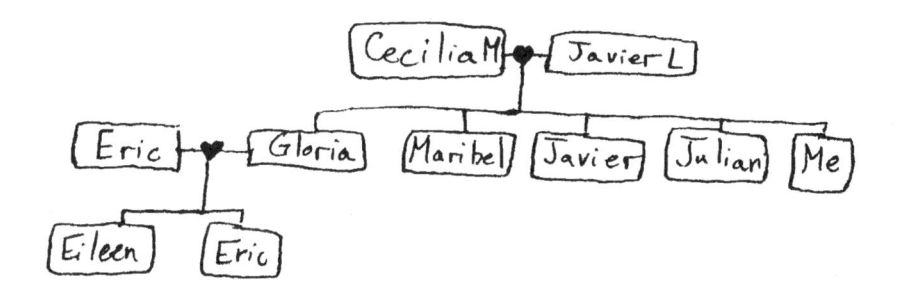

```
                    [Cecilia M] ♥ [Javier L]
                              |
  ┌──────────┬──────────┬─────┴────┬──────────┐
[Eric]♥[Gloria] [Maribel] [Javier] [Julian] [Me]
   |
[Eileen] [Eric]
```

Damn, my perfect squares! I'm the youngest of the five kids my mom had. My two sisters moved out, so now it's just me and my two brothers. The oldest in the family is Gloria. Gloria is twenty-seven, Maribel is twenty-six, Javier Jr. is twenty-five, Julian is sixteen, and I am fourteen.

Also, you know Mr. Patrick, right? He asked me if I could write *even more* for today's letter. Being the sassy me that I am, I said back, "Um, how bout no?" and my whole table laughed.

"I'm going to dye and cut my hair today, so I'll be looking G-O-O-D."

Do you have Netflix? If you do, you should watch this movie called *The Beauty Inside*. It's really funny and it's a romance.

What time do you make yourself breakfast? I make myself breakfast at around 8 or 9 p.m. Yeah, that's right, at night! If you hear a pan sizzling at night, it's fine. That's just me.

Last night, I was making myself some nice bacon, eggs, and toast when it started to smell a bit funky. My mom started complaining about it, and do you know what she did?! She threw a jar of water in my food and killed my toast! My poor toast . . .

Did you do the "Who were you? / Who are you? / Who do you want to be?" activity from class with 826CHI? Which question did you find the most difficult to answer? I didn't really know enough to answer the third question. I don't know who I want to be in the future, other than a student and a lawyer.

What did you think of Trump's inauguration? I can't believe that we chose an internet troll as our president. Do people think electing a president is a joke?! Do people not realize this has a huge impact on all future generations? Why do people want a racist, sexist, perverted old man as our president? This is the main reason why I hate people. They make such stupid choices.

Did you participate in the Women's March? I would've like to go but I had to go to a high school interview. Do you know Senn High School? I went up there for an interview. They were going to look at my art. When I was going through downtown on the train, I saw a TON of people and on Sunday it was the top trend on Twitter worldwide!

So, this is the last letter, huh? How are things going with your sister? I know we didn't get into super personal stuff, but it was nice knowing you. I wish you luck in high school!

Yours truly,
Julieta

P.S. I'm going to dye and cut my hair today, so I'll be looking G-O-O-D.

Dear Julieta,

I had to ask Mr. Patrick about your sassy self, LOL. For the first time, I saw him smile and even laugh! I got to know more about you from him too.

About my sister moving in, guess what? She's leaving. Honestly, I'm not going to lie, I'm happy that she's leaving. I was not used to sharing my house with another family. In a way, for me, it was uncomfortable, especially with her wearing some of my clothes and not giving them back! That is one of the things that annoys me the most: when someone borrows something I own and ends up not giving it back.

Anyway, you guys are lucky you had a Valentine's Day dance. We had Homecoming, which I don't go to. I don't know. For some reason, I find it boring. I really hope you enjoyed yourself and most importantly had fun! What type of songs did they play? Of course, I'll teach you some of my "amazing" moves.

Hope eighth grade isn't bad and that you enjoy it because high school is so different.

Love,
Angie ♥
(Angeles Nieto)

ANGELES NIETO is a sophomore at Amundsen High School. She loves to dance to Latin music. She's the oldest of four girls. She loves strawberry and vanilla ice cream. During her free time, Angeles likes to go out to the mall or downtown.

JULIETA LARA, age fourteen, grade eight, attends Zapata Academy. They live a simple, boring life and usually spend their time inside watching TV and eating nonstop. They're incredibly selfish, stubborn, and the most introverted person . . . but when they see someone who needs help, they will not hesitate to reach out. They can accept the truth when, deep down, they truly believe it. They hate being alone. Oh, and sometimes they like to contradict themselves.

ADVICE FOR GETTING THROUGH HIGH SCHOOL (AND THE REST OF YOUR LIFE) UNSCATHED

- Never CHASE A BOY!!!! (pg 130)
- Stay humble, and always have positive vibes! (p 194)
- When you feel hopeless, I suggest that you hang out with people who only give good vibes. (p 205)
- You might have butterflies but believe, everything will turn out fine. (p 279)
- Be Kind. Always. (p 279)
- Never lose who you truly are for another person. (p 203)
- Joining a program in high school is great when you need support and people to relate to. They will be your family throughout your high school experience. (p 52)
- Don't let anybody walk all over you. Be true to yourself. Be wise, and always be as humble as you are now. (p 20)
- Never let things get to you and distract you from learning or getting to school on time. (p 76)
- Try the single life. ♥ (p 116)
- The best thing to do is just make a lot of friends and focus on your work. (p 67)
- It's nothing like in the movies. It's nothing to seriously worry about. You'll be fine as long as you can keep good time management. (p 100)

EMILY ESTRADA & ESTER ARCE

Dear Emily Estrada,

Hi, my name is Ester. I am an eighth grader from Emiliano Zapata Academy. I love school. I love to learn. Sometimes I am too lazy to do things in class, especially during last period. At the same time, it's fun because it's math. That's my favorite subject. Math is complicated for almost everybody, but for me that's what makes it more fun. I also like playing sports.

My hobbies? Soccer and volleyball are the main ones. I was born here and was raised by Mexican parents. This means my dad works really hard to maintain us. My neighborhood is small. It is for people who don't have much money. It's not that great. How do I describe it? So, my neighborhood is dirty almost all the time, and we have buildings that are almost falling over, but I can still live here. Also, Chicago has a lot of violence. That's why it's really rare when my mom lets me go alone to the grocery store.

Either way, I have some questions for you, if you don't mind. What singers do you listen to? Do you play sports? If you do, then which ones? What's your favorite subject? What are some struggles in sophomore year? How big is your school?

While reading about you in the survey, I found some connections. You really want to finish your work. That's me. Sometimes I am lazy, but I motivate myself. You worry about leaving your family, as I do. One day it will be okay, but it's scary at the same time.

Well, thanks for reading. I will love to hear from you. You have a great sense of humor. I love what you said in the sticky note. Thanks for calling me sweet. You are so nice! Hope to hear from you soon. I will love to see you in person. Well, see you next time, bye!

Sincerely,
Ester Arce

P.S. I love your handwriting.

Dear Ester,

When I read your letter, I got very excited. As you already know, my name is Emily Estrada and the high school that I attend is Amundsen High School. I'm a sophomore, and currently my favorite subject is United States History. I find this class to be the easiest out of all my classes to be honest. I love playing soccer and sometimes volleyball.

I was born in Riverside, California, and I was also raised by Mexican parents. I don't have a father. Well, I do, but I just never met him. I live with my mom and my stepdad. I have three sisters and one on the way, so four. I know what your parents are going through. Really, my parents are just the same as yours.

I would love to answer your questions: the singer that I listen to most would be Kanye West or Chance the Rapper. The struggle in sophomore year for me is taking quizzes. I mean, the school work is quite easy, but most of the time I don't do my homework. My school is about medium-size, I guess.

I appreciate you reading this and I wanted to let you know that I'm here for you. Well, I hope to hear from you soon. Maybe you can add me on Snapchat later. I would love to see you in person! Bye bye, sister.

Sincerely,
Emily Estrada

P.S. Thanks for calling me nice. You're like a little sister to me.

Dear Emily,

You're such an awesome person to express my feelings and my thoughts to. I don't have any fears about expressing them. Thank you for letting me feel that way. I got your letter and I couldn't take my hands off of it. When you called me your little sister, I was touched, and I felt a way I can't explain. I feel safe with you.

You talk Spanish, huh? Cool, me too. Well, duh, we were raised by Mexican parents.

Are you excited for your new sister? To me, that seems like a really big family. My family has five people: dad, mom, brother, sister, and don't forget me. What is the order of your family? For example, I am the oldest and I'm the responsible one. Then it's my brother and sister. I am sorry to ask (you don't have to answer), but do you know what happened to your dad? I found it really sad.

My dad is a strict man! In the afternoon on Monday, December 12, 2016, my parrot bit me on the nose while we were eating. I got him seven years ago and his name is Lovely. He's a Sun Conure and he is colorful—red, blue, yellow, and green. My dad threw him at his cage and hit him. I didn't know what to feel: angry, sad, or frustrated. My dad is a nice man, but if you get him mad, you get him mad. What he did went way too far. I disliked it.

I would love to listen to your music to see how it is. I see that you are a lazy girl. Well, me too! Once I was watching a movie and got bored of it. So, I wanted to change it, but the remote control was around five hundred feet away. (No, in reality, it was two feet away.) So, I didn't get the remote until finally my brother came down the hall and I called to ask him to get me the remote. That's how lazy I am.

Changing topic

What do you think of the word *freedom*? I think of it as having your own responsibilities, not having other people tell you what to do. You get me? Like you need to do everything all yourself. I think that's freedom.

You have questions? Well, give me questions because I want to tell you more about myself.

Bye bye, big sister.

Sincerely,
Ester Arce

P.S. LOL. We'll soon have our Snapchat! Let's just wait ;). Thanks for being there for me! See you soon! :P

Dear Ester,

You should never be afraid to express your feelings, especially towards me, EVER! You know you can tell me anything! (Unless you don't want to, then you don't have to.) I'm always going to be here for you. I care about you as if you were really one of my sisters, and you're just from another mother. LOL. I'm glad you feel that way. I feel safe with you, too.

Yeah, I'm half Mexican and half Guatemalan. My mom's side is Mexican and my dad's Guatemalan. I usually get called *guera* because the skin that I have is pale. Well, I'm not that pale. I'm almost the color of sand. Since I don't speak that much Spanish, I need to practice.

I mean, half of me is happy that I'm having a new sister, but the other half is not because I don't really like the guy. And yeah, I do have a pretty big family. My family is six people, soon to be seven: stepdad, mother, sister (eighteen), me (sixteen), sister (twelve), and sister (seven). To be honest, I wish I were the oldest.

I never met my birth father. All I know is that the day I was born he told my mom that he wanted a DNA test. He didn't believe I was his daughter because of my skin color.

All the guys that my mom has been with are completely mean. I really don't know why my mom goes for guys like that. That's why when I'm dating, I try not to choose guys like them. I don't want to follow in her footsteps. But anyway, I feel you. My parents are strict too. People say that having strict parents is better than having parents who are not, because they don't see that their children are doing really bad stuff outside on the streets. They do things like drugs, steal, disrespect, come home late, have sex, ditch school, and do things they're not allowed to do on social media. Sometimes they don't get caught doing bad things like this, but when they do, their parents don't seem to care or punish them. They're just going to keep doing the same thing, but when they get older, they're going to hate their parents for not being stricter. But to be honest, I do want a little more freedom.

I had a bird too. We had to get rid of it because apparently there were complaints about our bird making way too much noise. Our bird did make so much noise. My bird was a Sun Conure parakeet also. His name was Mango because the color of his feathers was yellowish, like a mango. LOL.

I like the song "Nothing is Promised" by Rihanna. I'm so lazy that when I get out of school that I'll take the bus even if it takes me four minutes to walk to the train. When I'm hungry, I sometimes send one of my sisters to get me food. When I'm cleaning, I usually pick up with my feet because I'm too lazy to bend down. LOL.

I want to know more about you, so I have some questions to ask you. What kind of stores do you shop at for clothing? Do you wear makeup? If so, where do you get your makeup from? What color is your hair? What kind of shoes do you own? Do you prefer Dr. Pepper or Pepsi to drink? I hope you don't mind me asking these questions. *Te amo* ♥.

Sincerely,
Tu hermana Emily :)

Hola, Big Sis,

For you, my friend, I write a letter. To describe myself: I am almost everyday wearing skirts, and my hair is brown. I don't use much makeup, but I love it. I'm a tomboy but not exactly. I love to draw, but I draw kind of anime characters. My family, as you may know, are five: mom, dad, my brother (ten), my sister (eight), and me. It's so hard to win an argument with my sister because moms always go with the smallest kid because they seem innocent. Believe me, my sister is not innocent.

To add on to the makeup: my mom used to have a lot of makeup, but she threw it away because she didn't know how to use it.

For my type of shoes: I like Converse or Nikes if they are on sale at Carson's and JCPenny.

I haven't tasted Dr. Pepper in the longest time, so I'll choose Pepsi.

I agree that having strict parents is best because my mom makes me stronger for my future.

After reading your whole letter, I think that you are a strong girl. Don't worry, sometimes what happens to us is for us to remember and for us to learn a lesson. Have you dated someone? Or, are you not ready? I haven't dated anyone yet. I admire you for how strong you are. Keep this up.

By the way I love! MATH!

Well, see you in June. *Cries.* Time flies, so tomorrow we see each other. Bye and see ya! *Cries some more.*

Yours,
Ester A.

P.S. I have told you a thousand times, but I love your writing.

Hello my love,

How are you doing? Girl, guess what?! *Estoy enamorada*! LOL.

You're so right, but people like me don't deserve to go through this, you know. Everyone deserves to be happy and free. Most of all, they should feel safe.

I've dated someone who was exactly the same as my mom's husband. Sometimes I remind myself that I do deserve to be happy and free and safe. I celebrate myself by listening to music, taking walks in the park, and goofing around with my sisters and friends.

THANK YOU SO MUCH! I will keep being strong. You're so sweet. Can't wait to see you, beautiful!

Sincerely,
Emily Estrada ♥

P.S. Thank you again. Your handwriting is nice too.

EMILY ESTRADA is a sophomore in Chicago. She wants to become a professional makeup artist and model. She enjoys spending time with her family and friends. Emily likes to learn and help others in need. She's trustworthy and amazing!

ESTER ARCE is currently fourteen years old and has lived in Chicago her entire life. She loves travel and hopes to visit England, France, and Mexico. She has Mexican parents who she truly loves and a whole family that cares for each other. She is shy, but when it comes to math, she is extremely active. She loves to read and learn, and also likes to play video games (her favorite is *Five Nights at Freddy's*). She dislikes seeing people sad and will do anything to help them out. In the future, she would love to become an architect.

EDUARDO VARGAS & BRAYAN JIMENEZ

Dear Eduardo,

Hello. I would like to know more about you. In high school, do you play any sports or are you in any clubs? What I like to do every day is eat, read, and do homework. When I'm done with homework I will be having free time and will hang out with friends. My favorite food is tacos. What is the hardest part of high school?

Sincerely,
Brayan Jimenez

Dear Brayan,

I just got your letter. What's good? How's school going for you? If it is going well, then lucky you. I've kind of been struggling with my grades and that's bad. But you know, I am trying to do my best for the most part. Just got to bring a few grades up. Yes, I've been studying, in case you were wondering. I guess I will have to try harder.

I actually do play a sport and that's baseball. It's been my favorite sport since I was thirteen. My stepdad taught me how to play. Any kind of position, especially pitching, is good for me. Although I don't play for my school team, it's still fun to play. My favorite team is the Chicago Cubs! Do you like baseball? Another thing I want to tell you is that I like to do homework too. It only depends on what subject it is. Social studies is my favorite. After school, I like to hang out with friends and play baseball at the park.

Anyway, to change the topic, I actually moved to Chicago on October 4. I used to live in Indiana, but stuff happened. My mom and stepdad got a divorce, so we moved here to Chicago. It is what it is. I didn't really feel anything and I am still myself. When they got a divorce, they put the house up for sale. Hopefully someone looks into it and buys it.

I miss my old friends and my old dogs in Indiana, but it's whatever. Ever since I moved here to Chicago, it's actually been really fun. There's more stuff to do here. So far, I've been happy. I still keep in touch with some of my friends. I text and call them, but I barely see them anymore. It's pretty sad, but the good thing is that I've already made a lot of friends at my new school. It was actually easy to make new friends. You just got to talk to people.

Well, I'm done writing. It seems you and I do share some things in common, which is great! Peace!

Sincerely,
Eduardo Vargas

Dear Eduardo,

I am doing a little bit good in school. I try my best because I know eighth grade is important, but my grades are not doing that good. I know that the grades matter for high school. For me, thinking about high school makes me feel bad and nervous.

One thing that is cool is that my soccer team won first place in the championship! We got special shirts to celebrate. We had a great time. It was my first team and first championship.

I like soccer because my dad got me into it. We would watch it on TV and play *FIFA* on Xbox. One day, I sat down and told my dad I wanted to join a team. Then I did and it was cool.

The Best,
Brayan Jimenez

Dear Brayan,

I just got your letter. I actually enjoyed reading. Trust me, I can relate. I felt the same exact way when I was an 8th grader. I remember I would nervous and worried about highschool. But don't worry. You might have butterflies but believe, everything will turn out fine. However, all you got to do is work and that's it. Just bring those grades up. I know you can do it! Anyway, that's good that you won the championships. How did it turn out? Were you excited, happy, proud? I know I would. It's a really good thing that you have a dad because I don't. But to be honest, I don't really care. I want to talk about how it's like to live without one. To be real, me personally, I don't feel anything. My mom has been there for me since day one. She would be the one to support me with all the stuff. She's pu Puerto Rican like me. The food she makes is re freaking bomb! Her personality, is so funny. I have to go now. Be kind. Always.

Your buddy,
Edwardo Vazquez

Dear Brayan,

I just got your letter. I really enjoyed reading it. Trust me, I can relate. I felt the same exact way about high school when I was an eighth grader. I remember I would feel nervous and worried, but don't worry. You might have butterflies, but just believe everything will turn out fine. All you've got to do is work and that's it. Just bring those grades up. I know you can do it!

Anyway, that's good that you won the championship. Were you excited, happy, proud? I know I would be. It's a really good thing that you have a dad because I don't. To be honest, I don't really care. I want to talk about what it's like to live without one. To be real, for me personally, I don't feel anything. My mom has been there for me since day one. She is the one who supports me in all the stuff in my life. She's Puerto Rican, like me. The food she makes is so freaking bomb! Her personality is so funny.

Okay, I have to go now. Be kind. Always.

Your buddy,
Eduardo V.

EDUARDO VARGAS is a sophomore who is sixteen years old. Eduardo is a pretty outgoing guy. He'll tell you everything about himself. Eduardo is an outside kind of guy. He loves nature and anything that has to do with it. His favorite sport is baseball. Eduardo lives in Chicago.

BRAYAN JIMENEZ, age fourteen, grade eight, goes to Emiliano Zapata Academy. He loves to play soccer and win and also score goals. He lives in Little Village, a neighborhood full of Mexican people who love to eat tacos. He loves eating a lot and likes to sleep all the time. Sometimes he doesn't like to wake up and go to school. Some day he will grow up to be a police officer.

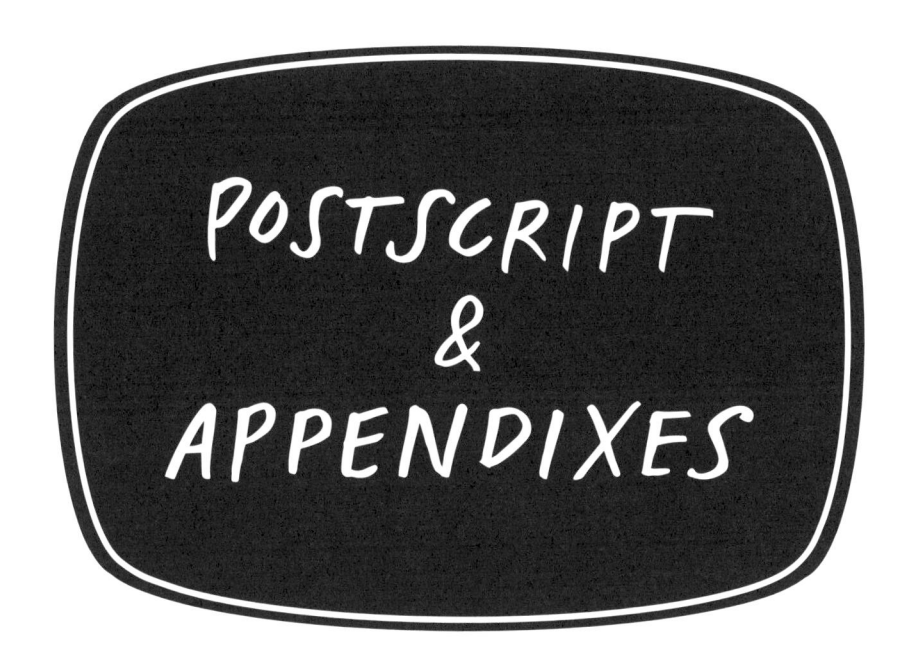

POSTSCRIPT & APPENDIXES

A POST-SCRIPT FROM AMUNDSEN HIGH SCHOOL'S STUDENT AMBASSADORS

P.S.

Thank you for keeping an open mind as you took time out of your day to read these letters. Even if you couldn't directly relate to everything within this book, we hope that we've at least helped you to feel what we feel, or remember what it was like to be in 8th or 10th grade. We hope our letters inspire you to meet new people, write letters of your own, and take risks to be vulnerable with others.

Letter-writing is something many of us hadn't tried yet. We usually text each other, or talk on Snapchat or Instagram. Once we got used to it, we realized we'd learned a better way to communicate with people. A letter won't disappear like a text, so we can remember every word from the letters that felt super emotional and personal to us. And, only the person you are writing to can see it! So letter-writing is a good way to express your feelings and tell someone your secrets without everyone else knowing about it. Also, life is basically just meeting new people. You have to get used to going out, making new connections, and putting yourself out there.

One of the most challenging parts of this project was getting started. Because we didn't know who our letter-writing partners were, what they looked like, or what their intentions with our personal information were, it felt uncomfotable to be honest—even for the most open of us. Writing these letters was like a gateway for us to start expressing ourselves. We had to ease into trusting each other, taking risks and being brave without knowing what would happen. Once we realized that our new friend was also nervous about spilling their emotional stories with us, it was easier to just release everything.

It was also difficult to revisit and release painful memories from our lives to strangers . . . but on the other hand, it was a little easier than telling our parents or friends or people we see on a daily basis, who we feel might judge us. Plus, meeting new people is hard, and trying to connect with them can be even harder. Taking away the face-to-face interaction by writing to a new person made it a little bit easier by taking away the nerves.

This project was such a great experience for our class. Some of us never thought we could be writers but toward the end we realized, *Hey, I'm actually pretty good at writing.* Some of us started coming to class more often because we looked forward to working on the project with 826CHI tutors. Some of us learned that we don't always have to keep our emotions in and put up walls. Some of us got to feel like role models for the first time ever, and realized it feels amazing and is really fun to be looked up to.

We also want you to know that Amundsen High School is not the place it used to be. It has been transformed. Now it is a special place because your peers and your teachers all look out for you, no matter what. They're there to help you achieve and to motivate you to work even harder. It's also super diverse—there are so many different kinds of people! Usually in high schools you'd imagine tons of crazy cliques like in Mean Girls, but it's not like that at Amundsen. If you walked into the lunchroom you'd see everyone connecting with everyone, and no specific groups for types of people. No football table, no soccer table, no LTBGQ table, no [insert any race here] table, no writing table. We all mix together. This allows for everyone to be able to meet new people all the time, which is so important because it helps us change and grow.

We, want to leave you with this thought: Don't be afraid to express your thoughts to someone, even if it *is* just through texting. Write or just reach out to someone. Tell your story even if it's scary. In the long run, you'll feel way better.

Sincerely,

SAMANTHA GUTIERREZ
JAZMINE RODRIGUEZ
SHIVAM PATEL
DULCE RIVERA
JAVIER TRUJILLO
HENRY MATTESON
MATTHEW GORSKI

AMUNDSEN'S TEACHER BIOS

ERIC MARKOWITZ has been teaching since the previous millennium. He's been eating pizza since then, too. He just wants to thank 826CHI for giving these students such a unique opportunity to write and write and write. Awesome.

TANYA NGUYEN is an English teacher at Amundsen High School and is proud to say she has taught in Chicago Public Schools for twelve years. She strongly believes in giving students creative writing opportunities where they can express their thoughts and views freely. She especially loves to read and discuss poetry with her students. In her spare time, she enjoys hiking, bike riding, gardening, and any opportunity to get in touch with nature.

CURRICULUM GUIDE

Dear Reader,

This year's Young Authors Book Project was inspired by Cheryl Strayed's book *Tiny Beautiful Things: Advice on Love and Life from Dear Sugar.* The letters that Strayed receives are open, honest, and real. They come from people putting themselves in a vulnerable position in the hopes of finding a sense of connection and guidance. Strayed's responses bridge her experiences to the letter-writers with thoughtfulness, caring, and SO much empathy. She replies to everyone by sharing pieces of herself and what she's learned in life. This kind of writing is one we wanted to have our students begin to cultivate. We wanted to see if today's students, in the age of emojis and social media, would be able to connect with one another through the "ancient" vehicle of letter writing.

When we brought this project to teachers, they were excited. They spoke with nostalgia about letters they wrote or received in their younger lives. These teachers saw the value of this project right away. When we brought it to students, it was a very different story. Our first weeks in the project were filled with confused looks and many questions about why we wouldn't allow the students to connect via social media. "How do you write to someone you don't even know?!?" This question was asked by many, if not all, of the students. We asked for their patience, and we asked that they be honest in their writing. They *had* to share their stories in order to connect with each other, and this is where the magic happened. Once students shared a personal experience with their partner, they didn't want to stop. Questions about connecting via social media ceased altogether and were exchanged for questions about when they would receive their next letter.

We realized rather quickly that deep, real connection with others cannot take place if the students don't know themselves or value their own experiences. We worked, discussed and wrote a *lot* about ourselves throughout this process. We read work with authors or characters who were also on this journey, or had found their way through it somehow. We've put together some of our resources for *you* to begin this journey for yourself and/or for your classroom—we hope you'll let us know what you thought of the book, and how your letter writing turns out! Maybe you'll even write us a letter to tell us about your experience? ♥

We'd love to hear from you!

—MARIA VILLARREAL AND THE 826CHI TEAM

ESSENTIAL QUESTIONS:

1. Who are we? How do we want to represent ourselves to others? How do we tell our story?
2. How do we connect to others?
3. Can we connect to others through writing only?

ENDURING UNDERSTANDING:

1. The power of connection through the written word
2. My story and experiences allow me to connect with and understand others
3. Empathy is built through connection.

PRIMARY READINGS:

- *Dear My Blank: Secret Letters Never Sent* by Emily Trunko
  Crown Books for Young Readers, 2016

- *The Book of Unknown Americans* by Cristina Henríquez
  Alfred A. Knopf, 2014

- *Tiny Beautiful Things: Advice on Love and Life from Dear Sugar*
  by Cheryl Strayed
  Vintage, 2012

- *Letters of Note: An Eclectic Collection of Correspondence Deserving of a Wider Audience* by Shaun Usher
  Chronicles of Note, 2014

- *Love Letters to the Dead* by Ava Dellaria
  Farrar, Straus and Giroux, 2014

- "I Used to be Much Much Darker" — Poem by Francisco X. Alarcón

- *I Remember Slow Dancing with You*
  Memoirs by 9th graders from Bowen High School
  826CHI, 2017

- "What do you Really Want?" — Poem by Yerika Reyes
  Compendium III, 826CHI, 2012

PEOPLE AND ORGANIZATIONS:
Najwa Zebian — *Finding Home Through Poetry* — TedTalk

INTERACTING WITH THIS BOOK

Many of the writing prompts we utilized during our time in the classroom are in this book. You can use them in almost any order to begin a reflective journey and/or to jumpstart student writing.

- Write your own response to any letter in the book.

- Write out the advice you would give someone in the book.

- Send someone a letter. Start a letter writing campaign in your class/school with another class/school in Chicago or even another city!

- Write your thoughts down about how people communicate today. Is texting the best way? What are the pros and cons of texting? What are the pros and cons of letter writing?

- Imagine what the future of communication will be. Write what you envision.

- Write us a letter! Tell us about your experience with this book.

You can mail it to 1276 N Milwaukee Avenue, Chicago IL, 60622, USA

COMMON CORE ALIGNMENT

Reading: Literature

CCSS.ELA-LITERACY.RL.8.1 Cite the textual evidence that most strongly supports an analysis of what the text says explicitly as well as inferences drawn from the text.

CCSS.ELA-LITERACY.RL.8.2 Determine a theme or central idea of a text and analyze its development over the course of the text, including its relationship to the characters, setting, and plot; provide an objective summary of the text.

CCSS.ELA-LITERACY.RL.8.3 Analyze how particular lines of dialogue or incidents in a story or drama propel the action, reveal aspects of a character, or provoke a decision.

CCSS.ELA-LITERACY.RL.9-10.1 Cite strong and thorough textual evidence to support analysis of what the text says explicitly as well as inferences drawn from the text.

CCSS.ELA-LITERACY.RL.9-10.2 Determine a theme or central idea of a text and analyze in detail its development over the course of the text, including how it emerges and is shaped and refined by specific details; provide an objective summary of the text.

CCSS.ELA-LITERACY.RL.9-10.3 Analyze how complex characters (e.g., those with multiple or conflicting motivations) develop over the course of a text, interact with other characters, and advance the plot or develop the theme.

CCSS.ELA-LITERACY.RL.9-10.4 Determine the meaning of words and phrases as they are used in the text, including figurative and connotative meanings; analyze the cumulative impact of specific word choices on meaning and tone (e.g., how the language evokes a sense of time and place; how it sets a formal or informal tone).

CCSS.ELA-LITERACY.RL.9-10.5 Analyze how an author's choices concerning how to structure a text, order events within it (e.g., parallel plots), and manipulate time (e.g., pacing, flashbacks) create such effects as mystery, tension, or surprise.

Writing

CCSS.ELA-LITERACY.W.8.2 Write informative/explanatory texts to examine a topic and convey ideas, concepts, and information through the selection, organization, and analysis of relevant content.

CCSS.ELA-LITERACY.W.8.3 Write narratives to develop real or imagined experiences or events using effective technique, relevant descriptive details, and well-structured event sequences.

CCSS.ELA-LITERACY.W.8.4 Produce clear and coherent writing in which the development, organization, and style are appropriate to task, purpose, and audience. (Grade-specific expectations for writing types are defined in standards 1-3 above.)

CCSS.ELA-LITERACY.W.8.5 With some guidance and support from peers and adults, develop and strengthen writing as needed by planning, revising, editing, rewriting, or trying a new approach, focusing on how well purpose and audience have been addressed. (Editing for conventions should demonstrate command of Language standards 1-3 up to and including grade 8 here.)

CCSS.ELA-LITERACY.W.8.10 Write routinely over extended time frames (time for research, reflection, and revision) and shorter time frames (a single sitting or a day or two) for a range of discipline-specific tasks, purposes, and audiences.

CCSS.ELA-LITERACY.W.9-10.2 Write informative/explanatory texts to examine and convey complex ideas, concepts, and information clearly and accurately through the effective selection, organization, and analysis of content.

CCSS.ELA-LITERACY.W.9-10.3 Write narratives to develop real or imagined experiences or events using effective technique, well-chosen details, and well-structured event sequences.

CCSS.ELA-LITERACY.W.9-10.4 Produce clear and coherent writing in which the development, organization, and style are appropriate to task, purpose, and audience. (Grade-specific expectations for writing types are defined in standards 1-3 above.)

CCSS.ELA-LITERACY.W.9-10.5 Develop and strengthen writing as needed by planning, revising, editing, rewriting, or trying a new approach, focusing on addressing what is most significant for a specific purpose and audience. (Editing for conventions should demonstrate command of Language standards 1-3 up to and including grades 9-10 here.)

CCSS.ELA-LITERACY.W.9-10.9 Draw evidence from literary or informational texts to support analysis, reflection, and research.

Range of Writing:

CCSS.ELA-LITERACY.W.9-10.10 Write routinely over extended time frames (time for research, reflection, and revision) and shorter time frames (a single sitting or a day or two) for a range of tasks, purposes, and audiences.
Speaking and Listening

CCSS.ELA-LITERACY.SL.8.1 Engage effectively in a range of collaborative discussions (one-on-one, in groups, and teacher-led) with diverse partners on grade 8 topics, texts, and issues, building on others' ideas and expressing their own clearly.

CCSS.ELA-LITERACY.SL.9-10.1 Initiate and participate effectively in a range of collaborative discussions (one-on-one, in groups, and teacher-led) with diverse partners on grades 9-10 topics, texts, and issues, building on others' ideas and expressing their own clearly and persuasively.

Language

CCSS.ELA-LITERACY.L.8.1 Demonstrate command of the conventions of standard English grammar and usage when writing or speaking.

CCSS.ELA-LITERACY.L.8.3 Use knowledge of language and its conventions when writing, speaking, reading, or listening.

CCSS.ELA-LITERACY.L.8.5 Demonstrate understanding of figurative language, word relationships, and nuances in word meanings.

CCSS.ELA-LITERACY.L.9-10.1 Demonstrate command of the conventions of standard English grammar and usage when writing or speaking.

CCSS.ELA-LITERACY.L.9-10.3 Apply knowledge of language to understand how language functions in different contexts, to make effective choices for meaning or style, and to comprehend more fully when reading or listening.

CCSS.ELA-LITERACY.L.9-10.5 Demonstrate understanding of figurative language, word relationships, and nuances in word meanings.

♥

Turn that awkward silence into a conversation with these questions from the authors

- What sport do you hate?
- Are you popular for your funnyness?
- Who is someone you hold close to your heart?
- Do you have a girlfriend? I know it's an awkward question, but I really want to know!
- Have you ever gotten into a cool interaction with a stranger?
- What are your favorite feelings when you play an instrument?
- What are some of your favorite conspiracy theories or urban legends?
- Have you had any wild times with your siblings?

ACKNOWLEDGMENTS

Throughout this book, you'll find that these young authors have written "♥" exactly 77 times. Their feelings for each other and the world around them were too great for the margins (and even the spaces between words) to go unadorned with symbols of their love.

We had every intention of carrying that sentiment into these acknowledgements: we tried dotting our *i*'s with hearts. We surrounded each name with several tiny hearts. We even attempted to watermark this page with one enormous heart, but alas. There are simply too many wonderful people who made this project possible, and we wanted you, dear reader, to actually be able to read their names. If you'd like, pretend this page is a red construction paper heart, covered in glitter, sprayed with our favorite perfume, and folded to look like a swan. Or, feel free to doodle thousands of hearts all over your own copy of this page. And now, it's time to spread some love:

First, we are incredibly grateful for the generosity of our donors, who fund our programs and publications. Thank you for giving our students the opportunity to become published authors and share their stories with the world. You help them engage creatively with their community and enrich the lives of their families, teachers, and peers throughout our city. This publication was made possible in part by Thomas and Christine Quinn, and Justine Jentes and Dan Kuruna.

This project—and the resulting book—would also not have been possible without the extraordinary trust and hard work of students, teachers, and administration at Emiliano Zapata Academy and Amundsen High School. We offer an enormous round of applause to Eliza Ramirez, Tanya Nguyen, and Eric Markowitz for joining us on this journey, and for being tireless advocates for their students and their voices. An enormous thanks goes to each of the 63 authors who participated in this project, with an additional high-five to those who penned this book's introduction ("Salutations") and afterword ("P.S.") as part of each school's student ambassador team. That means you: Marco, Jahir, Kayla, Vanessa, Santiago, Samantha, Jazmine, Shivam, Dulce, Javier, Henry, and Matthew.

An extra-special thanks goes out to the one and only Patrick Carey, our yearlong Publishing Intern who played a critical role in multiple phases of this book project. Every Tuesday morning and afternoon we'd find Patrick huddled over desks with students, encouraging them on their writing and emphatically discussing the smoothness of The Weeknd's voice. He helped us come up with thoughtful writing prompts to inspire students' storytelling, assisted in keeping 181 individual pieces of handwritten correspondence organized (no small feat!), and contributed greatly to the creative vision of this book. For all of the time and energy that you put into this project, Patrick, thank you.

Our sincerest appreciation goes to Erika Sánchez for her moving foreword, which acknowledges the tenderness and bravery of young writers telling difficult truths. For his commitment to amplifying students' voices through gorgeous book design, we offer a raucous round of applause to the endlessly talented Alban Fischer. Infinite ":) :) :)" to Julia Heney, who lovingly copy edited this manuscript to ensure that student voices rang clear and true, 24/7. And this ultra-sparkly-and-lovingly-doodled "♥" is for Cristina Henríquez, who visited our Zapata students to impart her wisdom and encouragement on all things authorly (during a blizzard, no less).

For spending their Tuesday mornings and afternoons in the classroom with us, individually mentoring students on sharing their stories truthfully and with flair, we offer an extra-special thank you to Marty Kezon, Patrick Carey, Carol Bean, Waringa Hunja, Christopher Howard, Doloria Ware, Ellen

Sawyer, Emelia Fredlick, Corey Palmer, Peter Batacan, Cara Suglich, Michael Schufreider, Colin Johnson, Max Silver, Jana Hartmann, Amanda Carpenter, Ivan Catudan, Vanessa Soto, Ross Kelly, Bria Berger, Janine Fierberg, Kelsey Rosen, and Jacqueline Ostrowski. We feel incredibly lucky to count you among the 826CHI family and are grateful for all you do.

We are nothing short of astounded by the talent and commitment of our 2016-2017 intern cohort, who supported this project in myriad behind-the-scenes ways: by photocopying, typing, editorializing, stapling, paper-clipping, organizing, and proofreading these letters. Our sincerest thanks goes to Waringa Hunja, Patrick Carey, Brianna Loomis, Lawrence Silveira, Alexandra Alvarez-Bright, Emily Lohman, Courtney Eathorne, Connor Shioshita Pickett, Lily MacFaydian, Peter Smyth, and Diana Fu for making this book possible, and for the countless ways in which they have inspired us along the way.

And, finally, to our readers: thank you for making time to value the work of these students. Within these pages are stories that rarely make headline news but are deeply important to the lives of young people. These stories deserve more space in the greater conversation about what it means to be human in this present moment, and we are grateful that you've played a role in creating that space.

If we can ask of you two favors: first, please make this book your own. You'll find ten writing prompts nestled within students' letters to each other; prompts that coaxed beautiful, honest, and meaningful stories from these young people. Whether you consider yourself "a writer" or not, give it a shot. You'll be surprised where your mind takes you.

And second, please do not simply read this book and place it back onto your meticulously organized bookshelf. Share these students' stories far and beyond by purchasing a copy for a friend. Or by reading it aloud to a stranger on the bus. Or by mailing it to someone you love . . . along with a handwritten letter full of your own thoughts and stories.

P.P.S. ♥

ABOUT 826CHI

OUR PROGRAMS

826CHI's free programs reach students at every opportunity—in school, after school, in the evenings, and on the weekends.

After-School Tutoring and Writing

826CHI is packed four afternoons a week with students in first through eighth grade working on their homework and sharpening their creative writing skills. Volunteer tutors help students with any and all homework assignments and lead students in daily creative and expository writing activities. Student writing created during tutoring is published in chapbooks throughout the year, and we frequently host student readings for parents, tutors, families, and the greater 826CHI community.

Field Trips

On weekday mornings throughout the school year, we host classes from Chicago schools for lively, writing-based Field Trips at our writing center. Teachers may choose from a wide range of programs, such as our Storytelling & Bookmaking Field Trip, which focuses on plot and character development, or "I Remember . . ." Memoir Writing, in which teenage students transform powerful memories into reflective prose.

In-School Partnerships

Because it can be difficult for teachers and students to make it to our center during the school day, 826CHI brings itself into schools across the city. Thanks to our dedicated volunteer pool, we're able to bring a team writing coaches to give individualized attention to students as they tackle various projects. Do you have an idea for a writing project and could use the assistance of 826CHI's educators and volunteers?

Workshops

Designed to foster creativity, strengthen writing skills, and provide students with a forum to execute projects they otherwise might not have the support to undertake, 826CHI Workshops are led by talented volunteers—including published authors, educators, playwrights, chefs, and other artists—on Saturdays and throughout the summer.

Teen Writers Studio

826CHI's Teen Writers Studio (or "TWS") is a year-long creative writing workshop that connects high school students to fellow writers, including peers and older professionals in the field. It's open to anyone in 9th-12th grade and welcomes youth from all over the city. TWS members meet twice each month to write together, talk about writing, and produce a literary chapbook each June. If you're into any of the above, this space is for you.

Publishing

At 826CHI, each student is challenged to produce their finest writing, knowing that their words will have the opportunity to be read, laughed at, wept over, or deeply pondered by their family, friends, and folks they may not even know. By the power of a very heavy binding machine, we are able to assemble many of the students' pieces into handsome books in-house. When not laying out, cutting up, and binding at 826CHI, we send special collections of writing (like this one!) to a professional printer with gigantic machines in order to put together a well-bound publication.

The Young Authors Book Project

We're proud of everything we publish at 826CHI, but we get particularly excited about our annual Young Author's Book Project ("YABP"), in which we partner with a local school to produce an anthology of student work. Over the course of a full school year, our writing coaches work individually with students to help them clarify their voices and polish their drafts. A self-selected group of students and volunteers form an Ambassador Cohort to co-write an introduction, and each YABP is also introduced with a foreword by a professional author. Every June, we release this publication to raucous applause at the historic Printers Row Lit Fest, where students are invited to read their work to an audience full of their peers, family members, 826CHI supporters, and strangers. These books are sold at bookstores big and small all over the country and are a huge source of pride for 826CHI and our authors. Flip to page 305 to read about our other Young Authors Book Projects.

The Wicker Park Secret Agent Supply Co.
826CHI shares its space with the Wicker Park Secret Agent Supply Co., a store with a not-so-secret mission. Our unique products encourage creative writing and imaginative play, and trigger new adventures for agents of all ages. Every purchase supports 826CHI's free programming, so visit us at 1276 N Milwaukee Ave in Wicker Park to pick up writing tools, fancy notebooks, assorted fake moustaches and other stellar disguises, books from local publishers, our latest student publications, and much more! Or, visit us online at www.secretagentsupply.com.

PEOPLE

Staff

KENDRA CURRY-KHANNA, *Executive Director*
OLA FALETI, *Student Impact & Data Coordinator (AmeriCorps VISTA)*
GABY FEBLAND, *Store Associate*
MIKE HERNANDEZ, *Communications Coordinator (AmeriCorps VISTA)*
ABI HUMBER, *Publications Manager*
MARTY KEZON, *Volunteer Coordinator (AmeriCorps VISTA)*
SARAH KOKERNOT, *Program Manager*
ESTHER LEE, *Development Associate (AmeriCorps VISTA)*
MOLLY SPRAYREGEN, *Program Coordinator*
TYLER STOLTENBERG, *Operations Manager*
STIEN VAN DER PLOEG, *Director of Development*

MARIA VILLARREAL, *Director of Programs*
TRACY WOODLEY, *Development Coordinator*

2016–2017 Interns
ALEXANDRA ALVAREZ-BRIGHT
PATRICK CAREY
COURTNEY EATHORNE
DIANA FU
WARINGA HUNJA
KINSLEY KOONS
EMILY LOHMAN
BRIANNA LOOMIS
LILY MACFAYDIAN
CONNOR SHIOSHITA PICKETT
LAWRENCE SILVEIRA
PETER SMYTH

Board of Directors
HILARY HODGE, *President*
AMY MCKNIGHT, *Vice President*
JAN ZASOWSKI, *Treasurer*
ALEXIA ELEJALDE-RUIZ, *Secretary*
KEVIN BOEHM
BRENDA FLORES GEHANI
VICTOR GIRON
RYAN HUBBARD
DEIRDRA LUCAS
ANTHONY MALCOUN
SHEILA PATEL
CHRISTINE QUINN
GERALD RICHARDS

OTHER BOOKS IN THIS SERIES

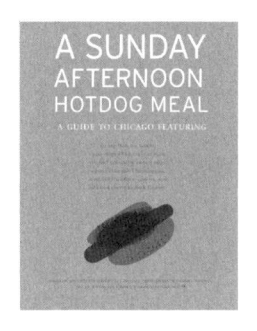

A Sunday Afternoon Hotdog Meal (2007)

More than two hundred second to sixth graders from schools all over the city wrote this riveting, uncannily informative, and often hilarious guide to Chicago. If you're looking for information on great places to eat, best practices for taking public transportation, or where to take a date (when you're nine), this guide is for you. This book can be enjoyed by those who know ketchup has no place on a hot dog . . . and those who insist that the sugary tomato paste does, indeed, go hand-in-hand with encased meats.

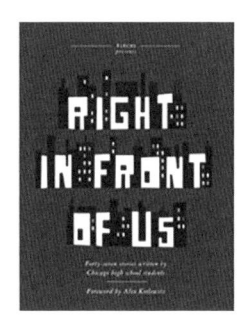

Right in Front of Us (2008)

Ninth-grade students at a Aspira College Prep spent a semester working on this powerful collection of personal essays about their lives. In the foreword, author Alex Kotlowitz (*There Are No Children Here*) writes, "These tales will surprise you. They take twists and turns that are unexpected, that are jarring, that feel, well, so real. You'll sense these kids' defiance, their hurt, their exuberance, their yearning to be heard."

Anywhere at Once (2011)

Anywhere at Once is a single epic adventure story told, collectively, by one hundred and six students (in grades two through eight) from twenty-five classrooms across twelve of Chicago's public schools. It pairs prose and narrative poetry with the illustrations of Chicago cartoonists Aaron Renier and Laura Park.

The massive combined effort of these students and dozens of 826CHI volunteers results in such marvelous tales as "How to Pretend You Are a Professor" and "The Best Brussels Sprouts on the Block." For readers young and younger, old and older, this wild adventure is not to be missed.

The Noise Felt Human (2012)
A collection of memoirs written by 13-to-18-year-olds from Gage Park High School, John Harvard Elementary School, and Golder College Prep, *The Noise Felt Human* features the moments, experiences, and individuals these students view as the most meaningful in their lives. Three teachers, more than seventy young writers, and fifty-three dedicated 826CHI volunteers came together to make this impactful and lively book, 826CHI's major 2012 release.

The Windows Reflect Everything (2013)
Narrative journalism meets memoir in *The Windows Reflect Everything*, a collection from the juniors and seniors of Golder College Prep and Roberto Clemente Community Academy. Within these pages, students share stories of heartbreak and falling in love, of encounters with police harrassment, and the challenges and joys of teen pregnancy. These stories will broaden your view of what it's like to be a young person in America, inspire you to reflect upon your own transformative moments, and brighten your empathy for these young peoples' dreams, fears, failures, and triumphs.

Even a Lion Can Get Lost in the Jungle (2014)
Even a Lion Can Get Lost in the Jungle features narrative journalism from seventh and eighth students at the Harvard School of Excellence in Chicago's South Side Englewood neighborhood. To challenge the media's negative

portrayal of Englewood, we asked these young people to tell us about the positive forces in their community that have shaped their identities. This book is filled with portraits of optimism in these students' communities, from an aspiring rapper who stays in school to increase his vocabulary to multiple teachers who have gone above and beyond to show their students how much they care. The stories are heartwarming, heartbreaking, and begging to be heard.

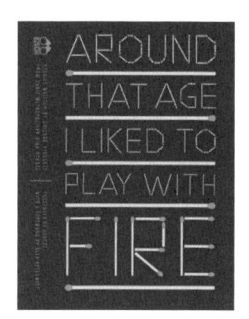

Around that Age, I Liked to Play with Fire (2015)
This anthology features more than one hundred personal narratives from tenth graders at Curie Metropolitan High School, and explore themes of *power* and *place*. These young authors have written about extraordinary real-life circumstances in bold and courageous prose, including stories of overcoming and transforming life's most intense moments.

The Monster Gasped, OMG! (2016)
This collection of 57 zany, adventurous monster tales penned by fourth and fifth graders from Brentano Math and Science Academy invites you to walk through dark tunnels, explosive science labs, and strange forests to explore beastly worlds unknown. Accompanied by twenty-four original illustrations by local artists, these stories will tantalize and surprise you. Among them you'll find the monster who wants a girlfriend, the Big Jelly Old Monster, and the Homework Monster. You'll also find a Monster-O-Matic guide to writing your very own monster tale.

GET INVOLVED

VOLUNTEER

We wouldn't be able to reach over 2,500 students across Chicago without our dedicated and caring volunteers. Whether by leading original workshops, providing homework help, designing the covers of our books, or copy editing manuscripts of student writing, our volunteers help bring our mission to life.

Visit our web site to learn how you can get involved in celebrating the voices of young Chicagoans: www.826chi.org/get_involved/volunteer

DONATE

Your donation makes a meaningful impact on Chicago youth and supports their development as they write their own futures. Your contribution to 826CHI goes directly toward our tuition-free writing programs, which include publishing books (like this one!).

Encourage creative thinking and writing here: www.826chi.org/donate

Or, mail your gift to:
826CHI
1276 N Milwaukee Ave
Chicago, IL 60622